Accent on Youth

by

Samson Raphaelson

with a preface by
John Anderson

SAMUEL FRENCH

FOUNDED 1830

New York Hollywood London Toronto
SAMUELFRENCH.COM

To

DORSHKA, JOEL AND NAOMI

PREFACE

It was William McFee who once defined the ideal book review as a frolic on the library steps. That engaging theory, if adapted to the published drama, should, I suppose, make the preface to a play a sort of romp in the theatre lobby. Possibly it should reflect the glimmer of electric signboards, suggest the bustle of happy playgoers in the glow of cosmopolitan bliss, the deferential snobbery of carriage starters, and capture all the pretty incidentals of a play's lifetime so that it would carry into its printed immortality all the joys it knew when it was on the boards, not between them.

But "Accent on Youth" does not, I think, need such artificial preservatives, even if I had them to give, since its essential life gracefully survives its translation from the stage to the book-shelf. This is not often the case with modern plays, since most of them are written so obviously to be spoken, and almost as obviously to go in one ear and out the other. They fill well enough the void which threatens the ardent playgoer between 8:30 and eleven o'clock in the evening, and they are really through when the curtain is down, as useless, the next day, as the stubs of your tickets.

This comedy, however, has a savor and a style which lend it a special quality in the theatre, and which, separated in the following pages from Mr. Gaige's brilliant production, identify this quality as the personal property of the author.

PREFACE

In these sleeveless times for a critic to say that a play has literary merit is usually taken as another, and more violent form of damnation. Oddly enough it implies the scornful tribute of "fine writing" in an art which, too seldom, achieves any writing at all.

It is safer, then, to avoid shabby inferences, to say that Mr. Raphaelson's play has style, and that, in Havelock Ellis's sense, his style is his viewpoint, and his viewpoint is illuminating, urbane, and witty. It is part of his craftsmanship as a playwright. He has as much respect for his characters as he has for his audience, or himself, and since he is writing about literate people in subtle complications of mood and impulse, he, being a literate playwright, turns them into human beings instead of mere stage names for a group of pleasant actors. It is the distinction between simply a funny play and a true comedy.

This matter of humor is close to the secret of the play's provocative charm and steady radiance. Mr. Raphaelson schemes out of his persuasive events a persistent, though unlabored, glow of amusement, knowing, as he does, that the inner smile is often most warming to the heart because it is nearest to it. His comedy is aimed at the heart, not the funnybone, so that its tear-strewn laughter echoes beyond the reach of the easier wisecrack. This quality, adroitly wrought into characters and dialogue, gives "Accent on Youth" its flavor and distinction.

Mr. Raphaelson has frankly made it a matter of record that when he first wrote the play he made tragedy of the idea of an elderly man falling in love with a young girl. It is further a matter of record that many a true word is spoken in jest. It is the truth of his play that im-

PREFACE

parts to it a touching and gracious integrity in the theatre, and it is the jest that enkindles it with the warmth of its humanity, the glint of its unerring comedy, and the wisdom of its viewpoint. The geniality of the play does not hide the fact that it also has something to say.

For this matter of youth is a monstrous and insistent myth in the world against which any competent challenger must lunge with the taste of sour grapes in his mouth. Our elders have shirked the issue, generations without end, on the cowardly notion that "youth must be served" with the curious and forlorn assumption, presumably, that the color of a man's beard is necessarily the color of his mind. They forgot that the absence of one might imply the absence of the other.

There are scores of wise saws and modern instances to back up the argument, proofs galore that there is no fool like an old fool, and that an old fool in love is a pathetically funny sight, the funniest, perhaps, except a young fool in love. Mr. Raphaelson is shrewd to make the distinction, truly witty when he puts it so genially into dialogue.

For it takes both to make the point, and to make it as pertinently as it is made in "Accent on Youth" in the face of a world that accepts youth, *ipso facto,* as a touchstone in modern life or any life. On a troubled planet, bristling with youth movements, this play has the poise and honesty to say that youth, as youth, isn't any better than age, as age. It says cleverly and sharply that it depends, as other human matters depend, upon the person who is old or young. It is no special and peculiar fate—like being able to wiggle your ears.

PREFACE

The very intolerant, which is to say the very young, may complain that Mr. Raphaelson has won his point in the play by making the young man out a perfect fool to begin with. But he hasn't; he has only endowed him with the essential qualities of inexperience. If that be youth, then youth must make the most of it. He has clung to the fair ideal that even the young cannot have their cake and eat it too. And he has given his young woman in the play the intuition to make the distinction. It is her choice, we must remember, the choice of wise youth, (wise not out of years, but out of bitter experience, which is the same thing)—it is her choice, I say, that sets a civilized though elderly human being above a handsome nitwit who takes setting up exercises. Love makes a fool of a man who already is one, and a wiser man of a man who is wise.

It is an easy thing for people to read ideas into an artist's work that the artist might disclaim in the detachment of his creation. And I am not one to belabor a bright comedy into moral Q.E.Ds. But if woman is the superman, the huntress, the predatory female seeking a fit mate for the improvement of the race, it must be a victory for the race when she chooses brains against the Daily Dozen. Brawn is no longer the immediate necessity for winning food in the world, (at least not at this writing), and if the thing is to be run above the level of the barnyard, Mr. Raphaelson is slyly convincing in letting us see that a wise peahen is not beguiled by all the sex strutting of fine plumage unless she thinks her mate has something besides his tail feathers.

He gives this woman, if I may be forgiven a bold comparison, something beyond Candida's wisdom, the humane

PREFACE

wisdom to choose the man who needs her most. That is a pretty and romantic notion, defensible on all grounds of sentiment and maternal impulse. But it seems likelier and closer to the arrogance of selection, if she chooses, as she does in "Accent on Youth" the man she needs most. It is this sense of equality, I think, this graciousness of mutual need, this notion that people have to be more to each other than biological mates to make biology humanly workable in a civilized society which give this play its point and edge.

You have only to ring the obvious changes on Mr. Raphaelson's plot to reach this conclusion. If she had tried marriage with another man of Steven Gaye's years but with more money, the point would remain true but banal. If a man younger than Steven Gaye, but equally clever, and charming, and congenial, had touched her life, she might have gone with him, and youth might have weighed out the difference.

But the point is that youth as youth doesn't lure her because—and here perhaps is the pith of the matter, youth isn't entirely a question of years on the earth so much as it is a matter of what you use them for. A man isn't as young as his arteries, or a woman as old as she looks, when it comes down to the business of living out a civilized existence. Neither is any older or, let us say, fresher than their ideas, a premise, I take it, which makes any dumbell of twenty older than Methuselah for all requirements of human society. In years all of us finally achieve the same age, which is death. What you think until then is your age.

James Stephens made that point with overpowering effect in one of his short stories—the story of a man of

∽ ix ∽

PREFACE

forty who, given a wish, wished that he might always remain his same age. In a veritable nightmare of descriptive narrative Mr. Stephens winds up his parable with the fact that that man died the same night in his sleep, to remain permanently forty, and to get his wish from the usually tricky Fates.

This was, I suspect, more than the physical aspect of that man's timely end. It was plain hint that the man could never be more than forty, and so I, for one, cherish the notion that he died of old age, and of natural causes—natural causes working in his own brain which told him that he was through.

The characters of Mr. Raphaelson's charming comedy meet and make their lives out of that knowledge, a knowledge denied, alas! to most people who build their lives on external fact. Mr. Raphaelson gives them the humor and courage to see what they are looking at, a stimulating endowment, full of grace and strength. Hence their tale, I think, takes on pertinence and human value beyond its obvious qualities of amusement, and hence, too, I stand here before it to say these things because it is a privilege to say that he has said them so wittily, and so well.

JOHN ANDERSON

New York,
March, 1935

⟡ x ⟡

STORY OF THE PLAY

In his early fifties Steven Gaye, famous for his comedies, has written the tragedy of an old man who loves a young girl. Although he is enthusiastic about it, he realizes that something is spurious in the construction. When he impulsively decides to abandon playwriting for good, and gives his young secretary notice, she takes her dismissal with ill grace. She blurts out that she is in love with him. As a man he is flattered and interested. But Steven has been a playwright too long not to have a detached interest in the problem of making life fit the theatre, and a large part of his interest in his secretary is the light she throws upon the problem of his play. By lifting his secretary's avowal intact he removes the one false note in his tragedy. He falls in love with her. Although she loves him, he is not without rivals.

"Accent on Youth" was produced by Crosby Gaige in New York City at the Plymouth Theatre on December 25, 1934, with the following cast:

LINDA BROWN . . . . Constance Cummings
STEVEN GAYE . . . . Nicholas Hannen
GENEVIEVE LANG . . . . Irene Purcell
FLOGDELL . . . . Ernest Cossart
FRANK GALLOWAY . . . . Ernest Lawford
DICKIE REYNOLDS . . . . Theodore Newton
MISS DARLING . . . . Eleanor Hicks
BUTCH . . . . Al Moore
CHUCK . . . . William Carpenter

Staged by Benn W. Levy; setting designed by Jo Mielziner.
All three acts are laid in Steven Gaye's study.

ACT ONE

ACT ONE

An October afternoon.

The study in the New York duplex apartment of STEVEN GAYE. *The room has many books, comfortable chairs and everywhere the feel of a civilized, individual personality. There are autographed photographs of actors, actresses and people in the various arts. There is a center door leading to the rest of the house, a door leading to* STEVEN'S *sleeping quarters, and an offstage anteroom, entrance to which is visible through the center door. We discover, seated in the room,* MR. GALLOWAY, *a rather elegant actor of about sixty,* MISS DARLING, *an actress of about fifty, and* DICKIE REYNOLDS, *an athletic, smartly-dressed actor of about twenty-six. All are silently reading play manuscripts.*

LINDA BROWN *comes in from the anteroom. She is twenty-six, dressed quietly, looks like a secretary—is a secretary. She carries a sheaf of letters and envelopes. She sits down at the library desk, takes a check book out from a drawer, and begins writing the checks to go with some of the letters. The telephone rings.*

LINDA. [*Into the telephone.*] Hello . . . Mr. Grindel? Mr. Gaye is out of town. . . . I don't know when he'll be back. . . . Yes, I'll tell him. [LINDA *puts down the tele-*

phone and goes back to her clerical work. Soon the telephone rings again.] Hello . . . Why, he's taking his afternoon nap, Mr. Benham. [*In a lowered voice.*] Yes, they're here. . . . Yes, they are. . . . I don't know—they haven't said a word yet. . . . Yes, Mr. Benham, I'll tell him.

[*She returns to her work.* MISS DARLING *rises, puts her manuscript down.*]

DICKIE. [*Looking up from his manuscript.*] Did you finish the whole play, Miss Darling?

MISS DARLING. Oh, no, Mr. Reynolds. I just read my own part. You see I'm not in the third act at all.

DICKIE. How do you like your part?

MISS DARLING. I adore it! I think it's Steven Gaye at his best—and it's such a comfortable part—I can be myself, a decent old-fashioned woman.

DICKIE. That's what I like about my part, too—just the word, comfortable. I'm good at sports—so is this fellow. I'm young, so is he. And everything I have to say sort of comes natural. I mean—after all, the public accepts me as romantic, and that's just the kind of part this is. Uh—Miss—

LINDA. Brown.

DICKIE. Miss Brown, you've read the play, I presume?

LINDA. Yes.

DICKIE. I haven't got to the end—but I get the girl, don't I?

LINDA. Oh, yes.

DICKIE. Who plays the girl?

LINDA. Genevieve Lang, I believe.

DICKIE. Oh, boy—that's impressive.

MISS DARLING. My husband comes back to me, doesn't he?

LINDA. No.

MISS DARLING. [*Surprised.*] No?

LINDA. No.

MISS DARLING. But he must. We've been married thirty years—he's left me for a young girl—the young girl goes off with a young man—he's *got* to come back to me. It's not a *comedy* if he doesn't.

LINDA. [*Drily.*] It's *not* a comedy, Miss Darling.

MISS DARLING. Not a comedy?—How long have you been with Mr. Gaye, my dear?

LINDA. Three years, Miss Darling.

MISS DARLING. Then surely you know Steven Gaye writes nothing but comedies. It doesn't matter how much the people in the play may suffer, the people in the audience always enjoy it.

LINDA. [*Patiently.*] Nevertheless "Old Love" is a tragedy, not a comedy.

DICKIE. I think "Old Love" is a funny *title.*

GALLOWAY. [*Who has been trying to read—now looks up.*] It might be to you, young man. It's not to me.

DICKIE. Have you finished reading the play, Mr. Galloway?

GALLOWAY. Not yet.

DICKIE. I get the girl, don't I? Have you got that far?

GALLOWAY. I've got that far.

DICKIE. [TO MISS DARLING.] If I get the girl, it certainly can't be a tragedy.

MISS DARLING. And an old man going off with a young girl —that's *comedy*. If you treat that seriously, it's dirty.

DICKIE. It's not dirty if you marry her. If an old man falls in love with a young girl and marries her legally, there's no law against that.

MISS DARLING. Try and tell that to a theatre audience.— And besides, *this* man doesn't marry the girl—he deserts his devoted wife and *runs off* with the girl. Everybody will sympathize with *me*. Don't you think so, Miss—uh—

DICKIE. [*Volunteers.*] Brown.

MISS DARLING. Miss Brown?

[*A pause.*]

LINDA. I hope not. If they do, the play will be ruined.

MISS DARLING. What!

LINDA. [*Almost maliciously.*] The audience should hate the wife, love the husband, laugh at the boy—

DICKIE. Laugh at me!

MISS DARLING. Hate me!

DICKIE. Have you ever seen me on the stage?

MISS DARLING. What kind of audiences do you think we're going to have—degenerates? To hate a good wife!

LINDA. [*Eloquently.*] *Anybody* can leave a bad wife. That's easy. *Anybody* can write a play about it. Everybody does But it takes a *man* to leave a *good* wife. And it takes a man to write about it. [*It sounds a little as if she has said, or heard, these same words before.*]

GALLOWAY. [*Rises, strides to the desk and slams down the manuscript. In resonant tones.*] Young lady, will you be good enough to tell Mr. Gaye that I have read his play from cover to cover—and that I have never been so grossly insulted in my life. [*He starts for the table, gets hat, stick and gloves.*] Good afternoon.

LINDA. [*Coming after him precipitately.*] Oh, Mr. Galloway—please—you mustn't go! Mr. Gaye will be in any moment. [*With sublime confidence.*] After he has talked to you about it, you'll get down on your knees and thank him for the greatest role of your career! [*This doesn't thrill* GALLOWAY.] Please, Mr. Galloway.

GALLOWAY. I couldn't trust myself to stay. If I played this thing, my career would be over. I've played butlers in my day, tramps, murderers, swindlers, and fools—but never a lecherous old man!

LINDA. [*Genuinely astounded.*] Lecherous! How can you say that! [*With exaltation.*] He's a glorious, courageous man standing just this side of sixty, surging under the last rhythmic leap of youth in his blood, rebelling at convention—

GALLOWAY. Young woman, there never was such a man.

LINDA. Yes there was—and is.

GALLOWAY. Where?

LINDA. Everywhere. The world is full of him. You're one! [*Picking up his manuscript and gesticulating with it.*] And if you don't play this part, Mr. Galloway—

[*The bedroom door opens and* GAYE *comes in.* GAYE *might be anywhere from forty-five to fifty. He has all the ease of a man of the world and all the susceptibilities of an artist. He is in a very quiet, grave mood. The moment he enters,* LINDA *stops short, pretends she was picking up the manuscript in her hand, and returns quietly to the desk, where she goes back to her work.*]

GAYE. Hello, everybody.

EVERYBODY. Hello.
                    Good afternoon, Mr. Gaye.
                    Hello, Mr. Gaye.

GAYE. Did Benham call, Linda?

LINDA. Yes, Mr. Gaye. He'll lunch with you tomorrow.

GAYE. Good. Got those letters ready?

LINDA. Yes, Mr. Gaye. I'm just finishing the checks.

GAYE. Fine. Well, my kind friends—have you read the manuscript?

[*Pause.*]

MISS DARLING. It's a superb tragedy. I love it!

GAYE. [*With mild surprise.*] Do you really?

MISS DARLING. Particularly my part. It's such a new attack on the old character of the mistreated wife.

GAYE. [*Still more surprised.*] Oh—you got that, did you?

MISS DARLING. Ah, I could read between the lines—a good woman, written faithfully—

GAYE. [*Gently.*] Right!—

MISS DARLING. —but to be played—well—how can I express it—would you say "unsympathetic" was the word?

GAYE. [*Very gently.*] Miss Darling, you're amazing.

MISS DARLING. I saw what you were after! I said to myself, "This woman must be righteous, and yet hateful." And—I don't know whether you saw me as Laura in "Quick Silver," but every reviewer said I was just poison.

GAYE. Well, Miss Darling,—you cheer me up. And you, Dickie—how do you feel about the part of Freddie?

DICKIE. I don't want to sound like a yes-man, Mr. Gaye, but it's the best comedy part I ever read. That is, for me.

GAYE. Comedy?

DICKIE. [*Worried.*] It's supposed to be a comedy part, isn't it?

GAYE. [*Softly.*] Yes—yes . . . But how did you find it out, my boy?

DICKIE. Why it's right there in the script. It's a relief not to have to play just another romantic kid—you know, audiences are getting tired of matinee idols—but now, to play a good looking—you know what I mean—

GAYE. Don't apologize. You're good looking.—Go on.

DICKIE. Well, what I mean is, to play a young fellow, but to show how *funny* a young fellow can be—that's something, isn't it?

GAYE. It is, Dickie. It is. But do you suppose we can ever get them to laugh at you?

DICKIE. Now you're kidding.

GAYE. No—no. I'm just a battered and bruised veteran of the theatre. I just wonder if they'll laugh at Romeo.

GALLOWAY. If they don't laugh at *him,* they'll laugh at *me.*

MISS DARLING. And if they laugh at Mr. Galloway, they'll love *me*—and *that* would ruin the play.

[*Pause.*]

GAYE. You know, I've been through the throes of nineteen productions, I've worked with more actors than I can remember—but never in all my life have I met three actors as brilliant as you! I want to thank you here and now for a new experience, no matter what happens to the play.

MISS DARLING. Oh, I think the play has a wonderful chance.

[*Pause.*]

GAYE. What do you think, Galloway?

GALLOWAY. [*Feeling his way.*] Well—I can't quite—the old fellow puzzles me. I suppose I'm stupid—

GAYE. [*Disarmingly.*] No—you're not stupid at all. The old fellow puzzles me, too. Please go on.

GALLOWAY. Well, take that love scene in the first act— where he tells the girl what she means to him—

GAYE. It bothers you, does it?

GALLOWAY. A little.

GAYE. I was just re-reading it in my bedroom. It bothers me a lot.

DICKIE. [*Courageously.*] *I* think it's beautifully written.

GAYE. So do I, Dickie. I think it's the best writing I've ever done.

GALLOWAY. I'm not criticizing the writing—I just wonder if I—you know, after all I *am* sixty—in fact I'm a little over sixty—and me making ardent love to a young girl and frankly admitting that my wife has never done an unjust thing in her life—

GAYE. [*Nodding.*] I agree with you, Galloway.

GALLOWAY. [*A bit flustered.*]—On the other hand, there's a poetic something in the play—and if a man can catch it with a high heart, with a grandeur of soul—

GAYE. That's what I thought when I wrote it. I'm fifty-one myself; I can smell sixty. And when you're sixty, you're an old man. Personally, it doesn't terrify me. I've had a great time: married, divorced, had sweethearts—no

children, but nineteen plays—not a bad substitute. . . .
If *I* behaved like that fellow, I'd consider myself an idiot.
—You see, I tried to catch the poetry of a man facing old
age. I tried the impossible. Poetry is young or it's no good.
I visualized a man with guts enough to be unafraid of seem-
ing ridiculous—surging under the last rhythmic leap of
youth in his blood. . . . But I'm getting my doubts. You
see—it all depends on the actor who plays the part. If he
can catch the imagination of the audience—

GALLOWAY. I've played Shakespeare, you know.

GAYE. And very well, too.

GALLOWAY. Gaye—I think I'd like to try it. I'm beginning
to get what you're after.

GAYE. [*Sadly.*] Galloway, I'm an awfully clever fellow—I
talked Benham into liking this play—the shrewdest pro-
ducer on Broadway—

MISS DARLING. That's fine. Then you can talk audiences
into liking it.

GAYE. That's not so easy.

GALLOWAY. It's worth trying.

MISS DARLING. Steven Gaye's first tragedy!

GALLOWAY. Frank Galloway, at the height of his—maturity, experiments with a new value!

GAYE. [*Irrelevantly.*] How's Mrs. Galloway?

GALLOWAY. Fine.

GAYE. Haven't you got a couple of children?

GALLOWAY. Three. The youngest is twenty-four.

GAYE. [*Handing it to him.*] Take a script home with you—read it to the family. Sleep on it. You do the same, Miss Darling—[*He hands her a manuscript.*] Read it to your—

MISS DARLING. I live with my sister, at the moment.

GAYE. Good. Read it to her. And Dickie—take it down to the tennis club and get some of the boys in the locker room to listen. See what red-blooded young America thinks of it. [*In the meantime they all have risen—*GAYE *herding them out.*] And then, in a day or two, let's get together again and see how we feel about it.

THE THREE. All right.
Good-bye, Mr. Gaye.
I'm sure we're going to love it.

GAYE. Good-bye, and thank you all.

DICKIE. [*Lingering a moment.*] 'Bye, Miss Brown.

LINDA. [*Who is folding letters—without looking up.*] Good-bye.

[*They go.* GAYE *stands quietly smiling at the door through which they have gone. Then he turns thoughtfully and drops into the sofa.*]

GAYE. Linda.

LINDA. Yes?

GAYE. Finished with the checks?

ACCENT ON YOUTH

LINDA. Almost.

GAYE. They can wait. [*She puts letters and checks aside and gets out her notebook.*] Got a script there? [*She picks up a manuscript.*] Read me the first-act love scene.

LINDA. [*Reads as he picks up another manuscript from a table nearby and silently reads with her.*] "I'm old enough to be your father—almost old enough to be your grandfather."

GAYE. [*Interrupts.*] I'll read it. You read the girl's part. [*Reads—with feeling.*] "I'm old enough to be your father —almost old enough to be your grandfather. I'm sixty. In five years do you know what I'll be? Sixty-five.—When I was young, don't you think I wanted you? You just didn't happen to be around, that's all. You came thirty years late. . . . Do you think I'm going to let Time cheat me? You came late—but not too late. I want the five best years of your life; but I'll give you my five best years for them. And when it's over, it will be easy for you—because I'll be too old to suffer. . . . And you'll be thirty."

LINDA. [*Reads—but is she merely reading?*] "I . . . I'll be a queen."

GAYE. [*Reads.*] "Think of all I've saved up for you—the accumulation of the years—all the trails I've traveled so I can show you the scenery—the wines I bottled so you can taste them now—the bitternesses I suffered so I could distill a sweetness fine enough for you. You'll be giving me your youth—but I'll be giving you my life." . . . Can you imagine Galloway saying that?

ACCENT ON YOUTH

LINDA. Yes, I can.

GAYE. So can I, as a matter of fact. But when you actually *see* him—or any other old man—

LINDA. It would make me never want to look at a young man again.

GAYE. No, Linda—no. Imagine Galloway alone in a room with Genevieve Lang. Imagine five hundred people peeking through the transom while he talks like that.

LINDA. I couldn't. They'd tiptoe away, ashamed of themselves for eavesdropping.

GAYE. Not when they've paid a three-dollar scale for their tickets, they wouldn't. They'd leer, they'd sneer; they'd think "the old boob, why doesn't he settle down in a rocking chair with his silver-haired wife and dandle his grandchildren on his knee"—and then they'd yawn, between dirty laughs.

LINDA. I hate audiences.

GAYE. You mustn't hate audiences, Linda. Hate human beings if you want to, but not audiences. People are drab, they're petty, they spend their days serving each other and loathing each other. But in the evening, after they have dined, when they get into street cars, subways and taxis and come together in the theatre, when the lights go out and the footlights go on—in other words, when they become an audience—they cease being human: they become divine. I am a playwright—life is nothing to me. It belongs to the workman, to the poet, to the politician. I worship at one shrine, the theatre. I must be true to one God—my audience. . . . What are you writing?

LINDA. What you just said. You might use it in a play.

GAYE. I'm afraid it's no good. A little too smooth and superficial—and besides, I really don't mean it.—Don't cross it out! You might as well type it. I may write about a smooth, superficial playwright some day.

[FLOGDELL, *the butler, enters.* FLOGDELL *has a distinguished bearing and is in his late fifties.*]

FLOGDELL. Miss Genevieve Lang is calling, sir.

GAYE. You mean—downstairs?

FLOGDELL. Yes, sir.

GAYE. [*To* LINDA.] Did she telephone?

LINDA. No, Mr. Gaye.

GAYE. Show her up. [FLOGDELL *starts. Thinking.*] Flogdell, has Miss Lang ever been here before?

FLOGDELL. No, sir. The last time we saw her was when we were living at the St. Regis. That was four years ago, sir.

GAYE.—Do you think we'll like her for the part?

FLOGDELL. I think she is eminently suitable, sir. She has unction, technique, she'll fill the balcony—

GAYE. In that case, shall we show her up?

FLOGDELL. Very well, sir. [FLOGDELL *goes. Pause.*]

ACCENT ON YOUTH

GAYE. Linda.

LINDA. Yes, Mr. Gaye.

GAYE. Suppose you type that little speech—and finish those letters.

LINDA. All right. [*She starts out.*]

GAYE. And, Linda—[*She pauses.*] Put in front of that speech what *you* said, "I hate audiences." And start my speech—"You mustn't hate audiences," et-cetera.

[*As he talks,* LINDA *scribbles in her notebook.*]

LINDA. I've got it.

[LINDA *goes out to the anteroom.* GAYE *sinks back on the sofa and starts lighting a cigarette.* FLOGDELL *holds open the door, and* GENEVIEVE LANG *comes in. She is a very attractive young woman, smartly dressed. Her face is neither too sweet nor too hard. She brings a play manuscript with her. As* FLOGDELL *announces* "Miss Lang,"—GAYE *tries to unscramble himself from the sofa.* FLOGDELL *goes.*]

GENEVIEVE. Don't get up. Just stay as you are. Now lie back, and smoke—and let me look at you—[*She steps back.*] and don't say anything. . . . What a nice room—and the nicest time of the day—and pretty soon I may ask for a cup of tea—but just now I'm going to enjoy the view, the books, the furniture [*Sits.*]—and the second nicest man I ever knew.

[*They smile at each other for a silent moment.*]

GAYE. Hello, Genevieve.

ACCENT ON YOUTH

GENEVIEVE. Hello, Steven.

[*Another smiling silence.*]

GAYE. Who's the first nicest?

GENEVIEVE. I knew him four years ago—his name was Steven Gaye. [*She takes off her hat and settles back.*]— What made you think of me for this part, Steven?

GAYE. Frankly, it wasn't my idea; it was Benham's.

GENEVIEVE. But you consented?

GAYE. Why shouldn't I? You're one hell of an actress.

GENEVIEVE. Thank you. It's one hell of a part.

GAYE. [*Suspiciously.*] *But*—?

GENEVIEVE. [*Earnestly.*] Don't you dye your hair a little, Steven?

GAYE. Yes. Can you tell?

GENEVIEVE. No. [*Suddenly.*] You're not married, are you?

GAYE. No, Genevieve. I'm a one-divorce man. [*They sit quietly for a moment.*] Pause.

GENEVIEVE. What?

GAYE. I said pause. I was mentally writing this scene— wondering when the plot would enter.

GENEVIEVE. You have betrayed me. I am about to be the mother of your child. If you don't marry me, I'll kill you.

GAYE. [*With a sigh.*] Ah, if it were only as simple as

that. . . . [*Pause.*] What ever happened four years ago, anyway?

GENEVIEVE. Now don't tell me you forgot.

GAYE. You never told me how you really felt. Did you hate me very much?

GENEVIEVE. Hate you? I loathed you. You broke my heart.

GAYE. That's nonsense. It's impossible to break the heart of a young, beautiful and healthy woman.

GENEVIEVE. I was insane over you.

GAYE. And I was absolutely mad about you.

GENEVIEVE. I don't believe it, and you'll never make me believe it.

GAYE. All right. Let's forget it. [*Pause.*] Now tell me how bad my play is.

GENEVIEVE. Well—the play is beautiful, but I don't need to tell you that. You write your women awfully well. Funny—that you should be so stupid about them in life.

GAYE. [*Annoyed.*] Will you listen to me once?

GENEVIEVE. What good will it do?

GAYE. It'll amuse you.

GENEVIEVE. All right.

GAYE. Now. We were all set to go to Paris—I had my steamship reservations—

GENEVIEVE. And I had mine.

GAYE. We were to meet at midnight on the boat.

GENEVIEVE. Right.

GAYE. At ten o'clock, as I'm doing my last bit of packing, I get the most hilarious idea of my life.

GENEVIEVE. You mean a *play* idea?

GAYE. What other kind is there?

GENEVIEVE. [*Sighing.*] Go on.

GAYE. All right. If I didn't write it then, while it was hot, I'd never get it down. Now, I'm not temperamental, but there *is* such a thing as inspiration.

GENEVIEVE. Couldn't you have sent a message, a telegram—

GAYE. *No!* . . . I got the public stenographer out of bed —*she* never forgave me, either—and I dictated until seven the next morning.

GENEVIEVE. You had enough sense to shut off your telephone, didn't you?

GAYE. I always do that automatically when I start to work. But there was nothing to keep *you* from answering my radiogram. I'd have come on the next boat. . . . What happened when you got my message?

GENEVIEVE. I jumped into the ocean and never was seen again.

GAYE. [*Cheerfully.*] Well, it's all over now, isn't it?

GENEVIEVE. Completely. . . . [*Dreamily.*] Steven, you really were a very attractive man.

GAYE. What's the matter with me now?

GENEVIEVE. You're nice.

GAYE. But not as nice as I was then, eh?

GENEVIEVE. Well, you're four years older.

GAYE. [*Piqued.*] So are you, my dear.

GENEVIEVE. When you're four years older than twenty-two, you're still a young woman. But when you're four years older than—

GAYE. [*Blandly.*] Forty-seven.

GENEVIEVE. Steven dear—you forget—you told me at the time you were forty-eight.

GAYE. [*More blandly.*] Did I? . . . I was lying—I was forty-nine.

GENEVIEVE. That makes you fifty-three.

GAYE. And revolting?

GENEVIEVE. Of course not, Steven. You'll never be revolting. But after all, fifty-three isn't quite the age to make a girl's heart go pitty-pat.

GAYE. Speaking impersonally—as an elderly man of the world to a young woman of the world—at what age would you say a man ceased being—well—just where would you draw the pitty-pat line?

GENEVIEVE. Roughly—at forty-nine.

[*Pause.*]

GAYE. [*Slowly.*] So that's what you don't like about my play.

GENEVIEVE. Your play can't help it—it's that kind of play . . . "Old Love."

GAYE. And I can't help it—I'm that kind of man—old man.

GENEVIEVE. But, after all, Steven—what's my opinion—audiences may like it.

GAYE. But *you'll* have none of it.

GENEVIEVE. I'm afraid not.

GAYE. [*This hurts.*] And none of me.

GENEVIEVE. Now, Steven!

GAYE. What are you going to do—wait for another play to come along?

GENEVIEVE. Maybe. Or I might just go away.

GAYE. Where?

GENEVIEVE. Anywhere. I'm mildly insane, didn't you know? Two years ago I suddenly just had to see South Africa. Allow me to inform you that South Africa is beautiful.

GAYE. Did you go alone?

GENEVIEVE. I started alone.

[*Pause.*]

GAYE. Have you ever been to Finland?

GENEVIEVE. No.

GAYE. Neither have I. I hear it's amazing—full of blue eyes and green trees and yellow flowers.

GENEVIEVE. And in the winter the air is so dry you can walk naked in the snow.

[*Pause. He comes over to her.*]

GAYE. Let's go to Finland.

GENEVIEVE. [*Smiling.*] What about your play?

GAYE. [*With feeling.*] I hate the damn play.

[*She looks at him intently. She draws him to her and gives him a long kiss. Then she looks at him with a little smile.*]

GENEVIEVE. I wanted to see what it would be like.

GAYE. How was it?

GENEVIEVE. Not bad. [*Pause.*] Do you really mean that about Finland?

GAYE. Passionately.

GENEVIEVE. Do you expect me to believe that I, or any other woman, could make you hate your play?

GAYE. Of course not. I knew the play was all wrong before you came.

GENEVIEVE. Steven Gaye, I don't believe you.

GAYE. [*Slowly.*] Will you believe me in Finland?

GENEVIEVE. [*Idly.*]—I happen to know that the *Île de France* leaves tonight.

GAYE. [*Thinks a moment.*] Fine! [*He gets up excitedly and goes to the door.*] We can change at Southampton. [*Calls.*] Linda!

LINDA'S *voice.* Yes, Mr. Gaye.

GENEVIEVE. [*Quickly, in a low tone.*] What do you want her for?

GAYE. Make reservations.

GENEVIEVE. I'd rather not.

GAYE. All right. [*Calls.*] Never mind, Linda.

GENEVIEVE. Never confide in secretaries. I once got into an awful lot of trouble through the secretary of a friend of mine. And besides, *another* friend of mine is an official of the French Line.

GAYE. Good! What time does the *Île de France* sail?

GENEVIEVE. Ten.

GAYE. Got your passport?

GENEVIEVE. Always.

GAYE. Can you get packed by ten?

GENEVIEVE. I can try.

GAYE. You're lovely. [*With feeling.*] Shall we, once more? [*They look at each other a moment—the edge is there: they kiss.*] Okay?

GENEVIEVE. Marvelous.

GAYE. . . . Heart go pitty-pat?

ACCENT ON YOUTH

GENEVIEVE. [*Stares at him, getting it. She steps back, shocked and smiling.*] You fiend. You devil. So you were play-acting—just to prove that a man past fifty could be—

GAYE. Romantic. Did I do it well?

GENEVIEVE. You had *me* fooled.

GAYE. [*Himself a little breathless.*] No—not really!

GENEVIEVE. [*Still shaken.*] Well—couldn't you *see?*

GAYE. Yes—but after all, you're an excellent actress.

GENEVIEVE. Good-bye, Steven. [*She gives him her hand.*] I'm sure you'll get somebody very good for the part. I've had a delightful time.

GAYE. So have I.

GENEVIEVE. Believe it or not, I was ready to go to Finland.

GAYE. Genevieve—this is absolutely preposterous—but I'm dying to go to Finland with you. [GENEVIEVE *stares at him.*] On my word of honor—

GENEVIEVE. As a playwright?

GAYE. No. As a gentleman.

[*They examine each other carefully, excitedly. They kiss.*]

GENEVIEVE. [*Really worked up.*] I'll get the tickets. I'll go right back to my hotel. What time is it, Steven?

GAYE. Why it's—my watch is slow—it should be—

[*At the same moment,* LINDA *comes in from the anteroom with a glass of water and a small paper box on a tray.*]

LINDA. Excuse me. Your five o'clock pill, Mr. Gaye. [*As she speaks,* LINDA *puts it on a table.*]

GAYE. Thanks, Linda.

[LINDA *goes. He stares a moment at* GENEVIEVE, *who smiles amusedly at him. Then he goes over, picks up the box of pills, and drops it into the wastebasket. He goes to* GENEVIEVE, *wants to embrace her again.*]

GENEVIEVE. [*Moving swiftly to the door.*] No—no. I must rush.

GAYE. [*Following.*] Will we have time to dine?

GENEVIEVE. I'll telephone you. Au revoir.

GAYE. Auf wiedersehen.

[*She goes.* GAYE *is alone. He paces up and down a moment. He presses the bell. He goes to the desk, sits, looks through a drawer for his passport, takes it out and sticks it into his pocket.* FLOGDELL *enters.*]

GAYE. Flogdell.

FLOGDELL. Yes, sir.

GAYE. I'm leaving for Finland tonight.

FLOGDELL. Very well, sir.

GAYE. Will you pack my things?

FLOGDELL. At once, sir. [FLOGDELL *starts out.*]

GAYE. Flogdell.

FLOGDELL. Yes, sir.

ACCENT ON YOUTH

GAYE. Isn't it exciting?

FLOGDELL. Very, sir.—At this time of the year, you will find the climate still mild in Finland. The days will be getting shorter, but there will be autumn flowers. I think you will require your complete wardrobe, for Helsingfors is a remarkably cosmopolitan center, and you will also find—

GAYE. [*Tenderly.*] Flogdell—

FLOGDELL. Yes, sir?

GAYE. I shall miss you!

FLOGDELL. Thank you, sir.

[FLOGDELL *goes.* GAYE *paces up and down again.*]

GAYE. [*At the door—calls.*] Linda. [LINDA *comes in with her pencil and notebook.*] Get Mr. Benham, will you? [LINDA *starts for the telephone.*] No—better not. He'll talk my head off. Take a letter. [*She sits.*] Dear Bill. When you get this, comma, I'll be on the *Île de France* on the first lap to Finland. Period. [LINDA *stares at him.*] Forget "Old Love," dash, and save yourself a lot of headaches. Period. Nobody cares about that old fool anyway. . . . What do you think of it, Linda? I'm quitting! I'm going to live! For the first time in my life I've stopped being a playwright—I'm a man, that's what I am, and I don't mean maybe.

LINDA. [*Reading—a little viciously.*] Nobody cares about that old fool anyway.

GAYE. Yes! Period. Bill, Bill, Bill, dash, I've retired. Period. . . . I really have, Linda. What a wonderful feeling! [*He*

ACCENT ON YOUTH

picks up one of the copies of the play and drops it into the wastebasket. Indicating a row of books on a shelf.] There are my collected works, nineteen comedies. I'm a success, and I've got money. Why do I have to write tragedies? You stick your head in the clouds, what does it get you— a crown of thorns. You put your feet on the ground, what does that get you—bunions. . . . Make a note. Advertisement. Apartment for rent. Eight rooms, two stories, view of East River. I've retired! . . . What's the last thing I said?

LINDA. [*Reads.*] Bill, Bill, Bill, dash, I've retired. Period.

GAYE. I've never lived before. Period. I'm going to do all the things I was always about to do. Period. I'll learn golf. Exclamation point. It keeps you out in the open air. Period. Then there's all those books I was going to read some day. Period. And all the people I was going to meet, dash. Think of it, colon, you could kill all the actors, writers and directors in the world, comma, and there'd still be fishermen in Capri, comma, peasants in France, comma, bandits in Sicily. Period. And I wouldn't be surprised if I found romance in Finland. Two exclamation points. . . . Why, Bill, this is something you ought to do, too. Period. To us Nature has never been anything but a set against which dramas have to be played. Period. . . . Just think of it, Linda! *I don't give a damn about that first-act love scene.* I don't give a damn about *any* scene. I never have to worry again about lines, characters, transitions, curtains— will *this* get a laugh, will *that* get a tear. I don't have to worry about audiences. To hell with audiences. I've retired! . . . What have you got?

LINDA. [*Reads.*] To us Nature has never been anything but a set against which dramas have to be played. Period.

GAYE. I'm afraid this letter'll be over Benham's head. . . . Kill it. I'll send him a radiogram from the boat. [LINDA *shuts her book.* GAYE *drops down on the sofa. There is a long pause. Very sweetly.*] And, Linda—you're discharged —with my compliments, my gratitude, my affection. . . . Now, we'll have to give you a nice present. What would you like most in the world?

LINDA. Nothing, thank you.

GAYE. Come, come, Linda. I'm serious. Would you like a car, a trip to Europe, maybe a trousseau? Haven't you got a boy friend?

LINDA. No.

GAYE. Don't be silly. You're a fine-looking girl. You'd make any man a splendid wife. Tell you what—write yourself a check for six months' salary. [LINDA, *after a moment's thought, goes to the desk, takes the check book out and begins to write.*] That's it. You retire, too! Here's an idea: go down to Saks' and order yourself a complete outfit. Charge it to me. Then take a trip somewhere. Take your mother along.

LINDA. I haven't got a mother.

GAYE. Oh, of course. I forgot. I'm sorry . . . [*With real enthusiasm.*] Take a girl friend along. Two nice young girls, Honolulu, ukuleles—Yellowstone Park, cowboys and Indians—see America first. . . . Or maybe Havana. It's romantic—[*She comes over and hands him the check with a pen. He begins to sign and then stops.*] What's this?—forty-one dollars and sixty-five cents?

LINDA. [*In an icy voice.*] Today is the fourth day of the week. My salary is sixty a week—four days make forty—and I paid a dollar sixty-five for that parcel post package yesterday.

GAYE. [*Puzzled.*] What's the matter, Linda? What have I done?

LINDA. Nothing is the matter.

GAYE. You're angry.

LINDA. No—I'm accurate. You've discharged me, haven't you?

GAYE. Well, uh—that's not quite the way to—

LINDA. [*Harshly.*] Yes or no?

GAYE. Why—yes.

LINDA. I have finished your letters, your notes, your telephone calls. You'll find everything filed away. All your manuscripts in order, all the bills for the month paid. The pencils are sharpened, the typewriter is covered, the desk is shut. My working day is over. . . . You owe me forty-one dollars and sixty-five cents.

GAYE. [*Hurt.*] My child, I owe you far more than that. As a matter of fact, strictly speaking, you're entitled to two weeks' notice.

LINDA. [*With cutting finality.*] You gave me a month's

vacation last summer on double pay—that covers every-thing. . . . Here's the check. [*She moves it toward him on the table.*] Will you please sign it? [*She tosses notebook into the chair and goes coolly and briskly to the anteroom. He looks after her, annoyed. He picks up the check, is about to tear it, then reconsiders and signs it.* LINDA *enters in her coat, putting on her hat as she walks. He is holding the check in his hand as she comes over to him.*] May I have it, please? [*Silently he gives it to her.*] Thank you.

GAYE. [*Still puzzled.*] You're welcome.

[*She folds it.*]

LINDA. —Now we're through—aren't we?

GAYE. Why—it looks that way.

LINDA. You're no longer my employer.

GAYE. No.

LINDA. And I'm no longer your—secretary.

GAYE. Right.

LINDA. We're two human beings together.

GAYE. Yes, Linda.

LINDA. A man and a woman.

GAYE. A man and a woman.

LINDA. [*Putting the check in her purse.*] Well—before I say good-bye, I want you to know that I love you.—I want you to know that the three years and two months I've spent with you have been the most wonderful, painful, happiest years I've ever had or hope to have. You hardly knew I was on earth—but you've given me more than you could have given your wife, or any other woman, or your friends, or your audiences. I had you when you were alone.—You've spoiled every man I know for me. You did that in the first month. I don't think I'll ever forget a single look of your face, a single word you said. . . . You've done a terrible thing: you opened my eyes and my heart—and you never touched me. It hurt—every bit of it hurt—how could it not hurt, it was so beautiful!—And if you think I can walk out of this house quietly—that you can smile me away with money and a few new dresses—if you think I can walk out of here without wanting to kill you, without wanting to cut my initials into every day you're going to live, you're crazy. . . . Good-bye—and *try* to forget me! [*She starts out.*]

GAYE. Hey! [*He rushes over and takes her by the arm. He leads her slowly back into the room. She is sobbing. Looking at her very thoughtfully.*] Let me look at you. [*Quietly.*] You strange creature. . . . You lovely creature. [*She makes a move. He takes her arm.*] Don't go away!—let me look at you some more. I'm not patronizing you. I'm *seeing* you. You're grand! . . . If I only were thirty-five, or forty, instead of—fifty-one. . . . What do you want of me, Linda?

LINDA. Nothing.

GAYE. That's not true.

LINDA. [*Breaking.*] I know it's not true.

GAYE. What do you want of me, Linda?

LINDA. I don't know. . . . Everything. . . . Anything.

GAYE. Sit down. [*He gently leads her to the sofa.*] Of course . . . Of course . . . Most natural thing in the world.—Where do you live, Linda?

LINDA. West Tenth Street.

GAYE. Apartment?

LINDA. Yes.

GAYE. And your parents are dead.—You went to college or something, didn't you?

LINDA. Three years.

GAYE. [*To himself.*] Why certainly. A girl like that—I come into her life—and it happens. Suddenly, like a banquet, she gets Broadway, literature, personalities, and me. . . . Linda, I know you won't believe it—but you'll get over this.

LINDA. [*Despairingly.*] Will I?

GAYE. Yes, you will. You're young, and you made yourself ready. The world is full of fascinating people—much more fascinating than I am.

LINDA. You know that isn't so.

GAYE. [*Slowly.*] I suppose there's something in what you say. . . . [*Turns to her with curiosity.*] Am I physically attractive?

LINDA. Yes.

GAYE. Funny, when you get right down to it, I can't think offhand of a man—you know—who *could* make you forget me. I'm beginning to see what a spot you're in! I *am* a unique combination—witty, sensitive, imaginative, worldly, gay—and yet with a feeling for tragedy. . . . And I know myself too well, I've been around too much, to deny that I'm charming.

LINDA. You're wonderful.

GAYE. Dammit—I know I am! . . . But, Linda, my sweet, I don't love you—I don't love anybody.

LINDA. [*Suffering.*] I know that. You don't have to tell me—I know that.

GAYE. And if I did love you. Suppose, for the sake of argument, I fell in love with you. It would be worse. Picture a man of fifty-one—why, it's like the situation in "Old Love" . . . [*He stops, completely smitten with an idea.*] Oh, my God . . . [*He turns to her, staring at her but not seeing her—springs up.*] Linda—[*Excitedly.*] Get your notebook. [*In a daze, she obeys, picking up notebook and pencil where she dropped them. He walks up and down the room in great excitement. She sits, waiting for dictation.*] Ready?

LINDA. Ready.

GAYE. [*Thrilled, boyish.*] God, Linda, this is marvelous! [*He comes over to her.*] How can I ever repay you? Do you realize what you've done for me? [*She looks up at him, bewildered.*] Angel—you've saved my play! [*He turns away abruptly and begins pacing up and down.*] Get this—[*She poises her pencil.*] It's a cinch, Linda. Why didn't I think of it before? *She* makes love to *him*—get it? How beautifully simple! *She* makes love to *him.* It whitewashes the old boy completely. God bless you, Linda. Happy? . . . [*She does not—cannot answer.*] I'm in love with the play all over again—aren't you?

LINDA. I always was.

GAYE. [*He goes quickly toward where she stood when she said good-bye, concentrating.*] Now let's see—you were standing right here . . . [*He dictates slowly as he tries to remember.*] "Good-bye, but before I go I want you to know I love you." [LINDA *now gets it. It's like a slap in the face —but after a moment, she writes it down.*] . . . Even the good-bye idea is great—what a build-up! . . . Do you remember what you said after that?

LINDA. [*She honestly tries to remember—after a moment, tears in her eyes.*] I can't remember a thing. . . .

GAYE. Doesn't matter. [*Dictates.*] "The years I've spent with you—" [*He pauses—glances keenly, impersonally at* LINDA.] I'm going to make her a secretary! Whole first act in his office—it'll work out—we can do it in three days . . . What did I say?

LINDA. [*Reads slowly in a controlled voice.*] "Good-bye, but before I go I want you to know I love you. The years I've spent with you—"

GAYE. [*Picks up the rhythm from her and goes on—very dramatically.*] "The years I've spent with you have been pure hell, every hour, every second, every day. Period. But

I'd rather have that hell with you than ten heavens with any other man. Period. . . ." Lousy! Too melodramatic. You said it better. I'm too excited. Kill that last speech. [*She crosses it out.*] . . . All right. Now let's see . . . [*He begins to remember a phrase—out of a great silent concentration he begins slowly to dictate.*] "You've done a terrible thing to me. You opened my eyes and my heart —and you never touched me."

LINDA. [*In pain and suddenly not writing.*] *I* said that! That's what *I* said!

GAYE. [*Groping and finding more words.*] "It hurt—every bit of it hurt. How could it not hurt, it was so beautiful. . . ."

LINDA. [*Still not writing—shaken, half to herself.*] I said that, too.

GAYE. "And if you think I can walk out of here without wanting to kill you . . ." [*He becomes aware of her— screams.*] What's the matter—aren't you writing it down!

LINDA. [*Managing to pull herself together; quietly.*] Give it to me again.

GAYE. [*Rapidly, trying not to lose it.*] "You've opened my eyes and my heart—and you never touched me. Period. You spoiled every man I know for me. Period. You did that in the first month." [LINDA *writes as he talks.*] What goes after that?

LINDA. [*In hell.*] "It hurt—every bit of it hurt—how could it not hurt, it was so beautiful—"

ACCENT ON YOUTH

GAYE. Got it down?

LINDA. [*In a shaking voice.*] Yes, I've got it down.

GAYE. [*Suddenly remorsefully aware of her, looks at her a quiet moment.*] Linda, I'm a brute—but that shouldn't be news to you . . .

[*The telephone rings.*]

LINDA. [*Rises and picks it up—into the telephone, trying to control her voice.*] Hello. . . . Yes. [*She covers the mouthpiece.*] It's Genevieve Lang.

[GAYE *hesitates a moment then comes over and takes the telephone from* LINDA. *He puts his hand over the mouthpiece.*]

GAYE. Linda, dear—do you love this play as much as I do?

LINDA. More.

GAYE. Do you think this new scene is going to make a difference?

LINDA. Yes, I do.

GAYE. . . . Will you type it? [LINDA *numbly nods her head and goes out to the anteroom shutting the door behind her.* GAYE *looks at the telephone with dread, then he plunges.*] Hello, Genevieve. . . . [*In dismay.*] You did? . . . Yes. . . . Yes. . . . The *what?*—the Bridal Suite! . . . [*Takes a deep breath.*] Well—I'll tell you, Genevieve—I don't know if you'll quite understand . . . No, no, no. Listen. You'll go through the ceiling when you hear this—but, on the other hand, it means a wonderful part for you—[*He*

43

stops as if cut by a whip. He stands stricken as he listens to a harangue.] Yes. . . . Yes. . . . Yes, but—[*Finally, in a defiant summing-up:*] Yes, Genevieve—that's *exactly* what I'm trying to tell you! [*Talking very fast.*] And all I ask is that you let me read you that scene when it's written. It changes *everything*—now listen, Genevieve, I switch the scene from Galloway to you—it's *your* scene, and at the same time it makes that old fellow as romantic, as colorful, as exciting as any—Genevieve! Hello! Hello! . . . [*With mixed emotion he puts the telephone back. He pauses a moment and then goes to the wall and rings for* FLOGDELL. *He puts his passport back into the desk.* FLOGDELL *appears in the doorway.*] Flogdell.

FLOGDELL. Yes, sir.

GAYE. I'm not going to Finland.

FLOGDELL. [*After a split-second's hesitation.*] Very well, sir.

[FLOGDELL *goes.* GAYE *stands quietly. . . . Now suddenly* GAYE *hastens to the wastebasket, takes the manuscript out and puts it on the small table, unearths the little box of pills, takes one of them and follows it by a drink of water from the glass which* LINDA *had put on the table.*]

CURTAIN

ACT TWO

ACT TWO

Scene I

A morning in May.

Same as Act I except there is a piano in the room, LINDA'S *framed photograph is among the others, one of the lamp-shades, hand-painted, is new, and all the furniture has been rearranged with a woman's touch.*

The stage is empty. The door opens and FLOGDELL *shows* GALLOWAY *in.* GALLOWAY *is in last night's evening clothes, slightly bedraggled. He looks sick and miserable.*

GALLOWAY. Are you sure Mr. Gaye won't be back soon?

FLOGDELL. He didn't say, Mr. Galloway.

GALLOWAY. It doesn't matter. I just came to use the telephone. . . . What a night, what a night! Flogdell—I danced three girls under the table. Would you believe it?

FLOGDELL. "Old Love" seems to have made a new man of you, sir.

GALLOWAY. But in the morning, one wants to go home. And one can't very well go home like this—I mean, one should telephone first, don't you think?

ACCENT ON YOUTH

FLOGDELL. The problem, sir, is what to say.

GALLOWAY. Precisely. I stopped in a telephone booth, and people stared at me—after all, I'm a well-known figure.—And evening clothes, at eleven on a Sunday morning, do not constitute a very good disguise.

FLOGDELL. Begging your pardon, sir, this is Monday.

GALLOWAY. Monday! Then where was I Sunday? Oh, Flogdell, I'm a very sick man.

FLOGDELL. May I suggest a cup of coffee, sir? For jaded nerves or any ills of the morning after, there is nothing so heartening, so soothing to the spirit as a fragrant, savory cup—

GALLOWAY. Don't advertise it, Flogdell—just get it.

FLOGDELL. Very well, Mr. Galloway.

[FLOGDELL *goes.* GALLOWAY *sits for a moment with his head buried unhappily in his hands. Then he rises and screws up enough courage to go to the telephone. He dials it. Into the telephone.*]

GALLOWAY. Hello, Annie. This is Mr. Galloway. [*In a confidential voice.*] Has Mrs. Galloway been trying to get me? . . . She hasn't? Are you sure? . . . Thank you. Will you tell her I am on the telephone? . . . [*Frightened.*] She *won't?* [*With bravado.*] Well, you tell her I've been sick two days at the home of Mr. Gaye— . . . She'll *have* to believe it! . . . [*He puts his hand over the mouthpiece and rehearses his little speech—with a superb air.*] Now, Roberta—as you know, we gave our last New York performance Saturday night. Well—after six months of an arduous stellar role, the sudden relaxation following the realization that I had a full week of rest before going into the Chicago run caused a natural collapse— What? How can you call me that—me, the father of our— *What!!* Roberta, you'll regret talking to me like this!—[*He takes his hand off the mouth-piece—in his original frightened voice.*] Yes, Annie. . . . She won't come to the telephone? . . . All right, Annie. [*A very frail, sickish old man, he hangs up the telephone and goes to a chair. In the meantime,* FLOGDELL *has entered with coffee on a tray.* GALLOWAY *turns to the coffee like a dying man and takes a gulp.*] That feels good. Thank you. . . . Flogdell, I've decided to stay here.

FLOGDELL. Here, sir?

GALLOWAY. I'm sleepy. I'm tired. Prepare the spare bedroom.

FLOGDELL. I'm sorry, but I'm afraid I cannot do anything so bizarre without Mr. Gaye's permission, sir.

GALLOWAY. Well, where is Mr. Gaye?

FLOGDELL. I don't know whether he'd want me to say, sir.

GALLOWAY. [*Desperately.*] I stand before you a dying man—cast out of my home, disowned by my wife—[*Suddenly shifting and in less feeble tones.*] And for what? Is it my fault that I have created a new romantic type? Can I help it if women fancy me?

FLOGDELL. These things are chemistry, sir.

GALLOWAY. Don't change the subject. As I was saying, you behold before you a man living in hell, who frantically cries to you, "Where is Steven Gaye?" How can you refuse to answer?

FLOGDELL. [*Takes a deep breath.*] I'll chance it. He has gone to call on Miss Linda.

GALLOWAY. Linda Brown? . . . Call her apartment.

FLOGDELL. I don't like to do that, sir.

GALLOWAY. Why? Who is Linda Brown? An insignificant little accident of the theatre—type casting!—Did you read the reviews? Did she get a single good notice?

FLOGDELL. She didn't get any bad ones, sir.

GALLOWAY. And I—*I* taught her to act. I sweated and slaved over her. And what do I get for it? I'm kicked out of Steven Gaye's house.

FLOGDELL. May I make a suggestion?

GALLOWAY. [*Dolefully.*] I wish you would.

FLOGDELL. Have you ever considered a Turkish Bath?

GALLOWAY. No good. That's what I told Mrs. Galloway the last time.

FLOGDELL. I didn't mean it that way, sir. I meant the act itself. The steam, opening the pores—[*The telephone rings. FLOGDELL hesitates.*]

GALLOWAY. Answer it. It might be Mr. Gaye.

FLOGDELL. Yes, sir. [FLOGDELL *goes to the telephone, picks it up. Into the telephone.*] Hello . . . Oh, hello, Mr. Schultz. [*To* GALLOWAY, *who has risen.*] It's the grocer, sir.

GALLOWAY. [*Sadly.*] Don't bother to see me out. [GALLOWAY *goes.*]

FLOGDELL. [*Into the telephone.*] Just a moment. [*He waits long enough for* GALLOWAY *to have gone out of earshot. Then:*] Hello, my dear! . . . Yes—I know—but you mustn't be angry, dear. . . . It's true—yesterday you were the butcher, and last week the laundryman, but, my honey-pot, we have each other. . . . Of course I do, I do, I do. But do you, me? . . . Say it again . . . [*He lifts his head. He hears someone coming. In a different voice.*] Yes, Mr. Schultz—a dozen eggs. [*As* LINDA *enters.*] Good-bye, Mr. Schultz. [LINDA, *in a street costume, looks extremely chic and expensive from head to toe. She comes into the room swiftly, aggressively, with pent-up excitement.*] Good morning, Miss Linda. Oh, I'm so glad to see you, Miss Linda.

LINDA. Where's Mr. Gaye?

FLOGDELL. He went to your apartment. Didn't you see him?

LINDA. How long ago?

FLOGDELL. About a half hour. He tried all night to get you on the telephone.

LINDA. I know.

FLOGDELL. And he went to your house twice—but apparently you weren't in.

LINDA. He nearly broke down the door.

FLOGDELL. He said he was *going* to break down the door this morning.

LINDA. Flogdell—

FLOGDELL. Yes, Miss Linda?

LINDA. Where did Mr. Gaye dine yesterday?

FLOGDELL. At home, Miss Linda.

LINDA. Alone?

FLOGDELL. Very much alone, Miss Linda. If I may say so, there was an air of melancholy about him, a strange brooding loneliness—and if you will permit me to quote Oscar Wilde—

LINDA. What did Mr. Gaye do all evening?

FLOGDELL. He paced madly up and down this room.

LINDA. Alone?

FLOGDELL. Alone.

LINDA. I don't believe a word you say.

FLOGDELL. I have told you the truth, Miss Linda—on my word of honor as a gentleman's gentleman.

LINDA. [*Softening for an instant.*] Please, Flogdell—don't be offended. I don't blame you for being loyal to your master. He's been good to *you.*

FLOGDELL. I may say, simply, that I would die for him.

LINDA. Yes, Flogdell—but suppose he didn't care enough for you to *want* you to die for him.

FLOGDELL. I couldn't imagine such a situation, Miss Linda.

LINDA. Well, it's happened! And I've come for my things.

FLOGDELL. Your things, Miss Linda?

LINDA. Yes. My things. There are seven photographs of me in this house. I want them.

FLOGDELL. What else, Miss Linda?

LINDA. What else? There's the piano, but he can keep that —that is, if he wants to go on with his lessons. But I want my pictures and my knitting—and—oh yes, this lampshade. I painted it myself—and he never liked it, anyway.

FLOGDELL. Is that all, Miss Linda?

LINDA. That's all.

FLOGDELL. [*Taking a deep breath.*] Well, I assume the responsibility of refusing to deliver the articles you name.

LINDA.—Then I'll take them!

[*She lifts the shade from a lamp on the desk, crosses the room and picks up her framed photograph from the library table. Thus, awkwardly laden and defiant, she stands as* GAYE *comes into the room.* GAYE *stops in his tracks at the sight of* LINDA. *They stare at each other angrily a moment.*]

GAYE. Flogdell.

ACCENT ON YOUTH

FLOGDELL. Yes, Mr. Gaye.

GAYE.—Get out of here.

FLOGDELL. Very well, Mr. Gaye. [*He goes. There is a moment of silence.*]

LINDA. I've come for my things.

GAYE. That's what I expected.

[*But neither moves.*]

LINDA. Well—haven't you anything to say for yourself?

GAYE. [*Astounded.*] Haven't *I* anything to say for *myself?* What, for instance?

LINDA. Well—for instance: good-bye—I don't love you— and I hope I never see you again. We agreed—didn't we? —to be brutal, to be honest, the moment the moment came.

GAYE. [*With weary bewilderment.*]—Are you crazy?

LINDA. [*Slamming down the lampshade and the photograph on piano and turning on him.*] Of course I'm crazy. Don't pretend you just discovered it. And *you're* crazy. That's why, when a time like this comes, we shouldn't lower ourselves to the level of sanity. I demand that we keep our hate on the same high mountain where you put our love. —Do you know what day yesterday was? It was the ninth of May. Seven months ago yesterday I was nothing to you —and you were everything to me.—You discharged me. I was willing to go. I told you I loved you, but it was an exit speech. I didn't ask for mercy. You pulled me back. *You* begged *me* to rehearse in your play. I never wanted to be an actress.—Well, I became an actress. Then, on the opening night, you said you fell in love with me. I didn't believe it. I knew you too well. And then—then I did believe it.— We promised each other it would be breathless and magical, or nothing at all. We swore, as we sat in the dawn, that the moment the glory stopped, whoever the glory stopped for would cut like a knife. You said, "The wonder that's in us is our love—and when that wonder goes, let's not live kindly, sweetly, disgustingly, with just each other." Did you or did you not say it?

GAYE. It's rather naively phrased, but I said it.

LINDA. Did you or did you not mean it?

GAYE. Of course I meant it.

LINDA. Then how could you—how *could* you—yesterday, on the seventh monthly anniversary of the day you discharged me—when I had bought a beautiful evening gown for two hundred and seventy-five dollars just for our dinner together—*how* could you break our date!

[*Pause.*]

GAYE. Did you read my note?

LINDA. Of course I read it.

GAYE. I think it was very clear.

LINDA. What was clear about it? You walked into my apartment at six-thirty—

GAYE. And I found your young leading man in your bed.

LINDA. And you left.

GAYE. What did you expect me to do?

LINDA. If you had the least bit of poetry in you, you would have waited for me to come out of the shower.

[*Pause.*]

GAYE. Would you have liked it if you had found me standing there?

LINDA. I would have loved it.

GAYE. You—you would have enjoyed explaining?

LINDA. Explaining? I should have refused to explain!

GAYE. That makes everything clear!—I find Dickie Reynolds asleep in your bed. I tactfully pretend nothing has happened, the three of us go out to dinner, and then, after the theatre, we all have a little night-cap, go to a hotel, ask for a triple bed, say our prayers, and turn in together!

[*Pause.*]

LINDA. Why did you refuse to answer your telephone?

GAYE. I thought that was covered in my note.

LINDA. —Why did you put the note on Dickie's chest?

GAYE. Oh, it seemed the natural thing to do.

LINDA. Suppose he woke up and read it before I came out?

GAYE. Oh, can he read?

LINDA. Beautifully!

[*Pause.*]

GAYE. Why did you telephone me if you didn't intend to explain?

LINDA. I telephoned to thank you for having put me in your show, for having introduced me to the world of the theatre, which I love.

GAYE. Then why did you refuse to answer your telephone when I called you at midnight?

LINDA. Because I decided I had nothing to thank you for! You needed me in your play, I made good, and you got just as much out of the whole miserable mess as I did.

[*Pause.*]

GAYE. May I ask you a question?

LINDA. You may.

GAYE. Why are *you* angry with *me?*

LINDA. I'm not angry at all.

GAYE. What do you call this—a laughing jag?

LINDA. No. This is despair—because your faith in me has gone—and . . . everything is over.

[*Pause.*]

GAYE. [*Slowly.*] I have all the faith in the world in you. . . . But I know too much about life, about women. You might be an angel straight from heaven, but so long as you're young and I'm old . . . I tell you there is no substitute for youth. [*Suffering.*] Every night, in that play, he takes you in his arms. Every night, in words that I wrote, his youth calls to you . . . every night—and two matinees a week.

LINDA. —You're jealous!

GAYE. Dying of it. . . .

LINDA. Couldn't you see the boy was drunk?

GAYE. [*Wildly.*] Don't! No matter what you say, it will be something I said in a similar situation.

LINDA. [*Coming over to him.*] Steven—

GAYE. Oh, Linda, Linda—

[*They embrace. They cling tightly to each other.* LINDA *cries a little. After a while:*]

LINDA. Steven—do you love me?

GAYE. What do you think?

LINDA. I think yes.—And I love you. I'm tired of asking you to marry me. But we must let the world know we belong to each other. Otherwise, why shouldn't a young man come to see me?—If you're afraid of the word mistress, let's say we're engaged. I'll never sue you for breach of promise.

GAYE. But I *want* young men to come to see you—every one of them. The field is free: that's the way I want it. I didn't buy you in a market place.—And you don't have to tell me what Dickie was doing in your bedroom. I know nothing happened. I'm positive of it. All night long I was telling myself that. The reason I called you on the telephone so many times, and the reason I went to your apartment, was only to tell you that it's all right, and please to forget it.

LINDA. Oh Steven—darling—let's never do things like this to each other again, shall we?

GAYE. Never! [*They are quiet in each other's arms.*]— Darling—

LINDA. Yes, dear?

GAYE. What was it Shakespeare said about men dying, but not for love?—Well, it might be true about men over twenty-five and men under fifty. . . . But I could die for love of you.

LINDA. . . . I'm so glad.

GAYE. I'm not. I see no peace ahead.

LINDA. Since when do you want peace?

GAYE. Since I've found adventure.

LINDA. Do you—really?

GAYE. No, I don't, really.

LINDA. I'm glad, because you're never going to have peace. You're an artist—you're never going to be middle-aged. You're going to stay young until suddenly one day you'll die, and on your death-bed you'll say to the doctor, "What am I dying of?" And the doctor will say, "Old age, you fool."

ACCENT ON YOUTH

GAYE. . . .Darling—

LINDA. Yes, dear?

GAYE. What did he do—just walk in?

LINDA. Who?

GAYE. Dickie.

LINDA. Oh, you angel, haven't I told you about that yet?

GAYE. Not that I can remember.

LINDA. He walked in unannounced, and very tight. I was surprised—you know, Dickie never drinks or smokes. And I couldn't figure out what he came for, because I don't think I've exchanged more than fifty words with the boy during the six months we've been in the show.—He talked about the traffic, and I talked about the weather—making a grand total of maybe sixty words—and then suddenly, like a gentleman of the old school, he fell asleep in his chair. Well, it got time for me to dress for dinner, so I went in to dress. When I came out from my shower, there on my bed was your note, and under it was Dickie!

[GAYE *brings a little jewel case out of his pocket. He gives it to her shyly.*]

GAYE. I was going to give that to you yesterday at dinner.

LINDA. [*Taking a bracelet from the case.*] Oh, Steven— it's beautiful! [*She puts it around her wrist and looks at it.*] I love it! Steven—we'd better cut out these monthly anniversaries: what with you buying me jewelry and me buying myself evening gowns, we'll both go broke.

GAYE. Will you live in a garret with me?

LINDA. I've always wanted to live in a garret. Just you and me—

GAYE. And Flogdell—

LINDA. And the piano. You mustn't give up your piano lessons—

GAYE. And when we get hungry, I can pawn my golf clubs, one by one.

LINDA. No!—they'll be the last to go.

[FLOGDELL *knocks on the door.*]

GAYE. Yes?

FLOGDELL. [*Entering.*] Mr. Reynolds to see you, sir.

[*For a second* GAYE *doesn't move. He turns to* LINDA.]

GAYE. Do you suppose he knows you're here?

LINDA. He's my lover—and he's coming to ask you for my hand.

GAYE. [*Smiles back at her.*] Send him up, Flogdell.

FLOGDELL. Very well, sir. [*He goes.*]

GAYE. That boy hasn't been in this house since the day I engaged him. . . . He might wonder what you're doing here. Do you want to stay?

LINDA. You bet I want to stay. And I wish, when he comes in, you'd say, "This is my girl—and what the hell were you doing in her apartment?"

GAYE. My dear, when you're an old lady and I'm your handsome young sweetheart, on that day I'll flatter you by branding on your forehead "Private Property"—but right now—[*Quickly.*] . . . Please—[*He holds the bedroom door open.* LINDA *hesitates a fraction of a second and then, blowing him a hasty kiss, she goes out into bedroom.* GAYE *shuts the door behind her quickly. The next moment the other door opens and* DICKIE REYNOLDS *comes in. Cordially but warily.*] Hello, Dickie.

DICKIE. [*Cheerfully.*] Hello, Mr. Gaye.

[*Pause.*]

GAYE. How are you?

DICKIE. Fine. How are you?

GAYE. Great.—Sit down.

DICKIE. Thanks.

[*Pause.*]

GAYE. Cigarette?

DICKIE. No, thank you. Bad for my tennis.

GAYE. Why don't you play golf, like me?

DICKIE. I do play golf.

GAYE. Oh, yes, I remember. You're one of those par boys, aren't you?

DICKIE. [*With a grin.*] I've heard about you, too.

GAYE. Well, whatever you hear, they're afraid to say it to

my face. . . . [*Watching him, waiting to hear the purpose of his visit.*] It's good to see you, Dickie.

DICKIE. It's good to see you. You don't get around to the theatre much, do you?

GAYE. Well, I'm pretty busy these days.

DICKIE. A new play?

GAYE. Hell, no.

DICKIE. It's about time, isn't it? Don't you write one a year?

GAYE. Oh, a fellow has to take a year off once in a while. I'm catching up on my education. Learning to ride a horse, taking piano lessons—

DICKIE. [*Grinning.*] I hear you're *good* on a *horse*.

GAYE. Do *you* ride?

DICKIE. Practically born in the saddle.

GAYE. Do you play the piano?

DICKIE. I had a band of my own at college.

GAYE. How are you on playwriting, you son-of-a-bitch?

DICKIE. Not so good—and I'm afraid I'm not an actor, either.—Mr. Gaye, I gave Benham my notice this morning. I thought I'd drop in and tell you so you wouldn't hear it from somebody else.

GAYE. What's the matter—don't you like to go on the road? Chicago's not a bad town, you know.

DICKIE. I'm quitting the theatre.

GAYE. Isn't that a rather sudden decision?

DICKIE. Well, I had a chance to buy a ranch in Wyoming —my father left me a little money—so I bought it.

GAYE. [*Wryly.*] A ranch? One of those places where you have to get up early in the morning?

DICKIE. Five A. M. Then wheat cakes, sausage, lamb chops, an omelet and apple pie for breakfast.

GAYE. You *have* to?

DICKIE. No. You *want* to.

GAYE. What do you do at night?

DICKIE. You sleep.

GAYE. [*Nodding his head.*] Sure—you're crazy.

DICKIE. [*Rises.*] No—*you're* crazy. Everybody in the theatre is crazy. I don't like them. I like good, sincere, two-fisted, straight-from-the-shoulder men. If I hadn't been in a dramatic show at college and if not for the depression, I'd never have got into such an unhealthy atmosphere. Everybody stuck on himself, jealous of everybody else, fighting about his billing, belly-aching because another actor gets more lines. All the men are a lot of show-offs looking in the mirror all the time. And the women are worse.

GAYE. Tell me about the women, Dickie.

DICKIE. They're unwholesome. I like a woman who falls in love, marries, has kids and makes a home. Am I right or not?

GAYE. You're absolutely right.

DICKIE. Sure I'm right. Where would civilization be if women didn't make homes? How is the next generation going to be brought up? Why, the women in the theatre, all they care about is getting emotional from eight-thirty to eleven every night, and then they've got nothing left to give to the generation of tomorrow.

GAYE. I didn't know you were interested in the generation of tomorrow.

DICKIE. I am.

[*Pause.*]

GAYE. [*Rising.*] Well, Dickie—I'm sorry you're going to leave the show—but I'm glad you found yourself before you became a character actor.

DICKIE. So am I. You know, most of us don't find ourselves until it's too late.

[FLOGDELL *enters.*]

FLOGDELL. Miss Linda Brown is downstairs, sir. Shall I show her up or shall I ask her to wait?

GAYE. [*Pause.*] Linda!—How nice! . . . Ask her to come up, will you, Flogdell?

FLOGDELL. Yes, sir. [FLOGDELL *goes.*]

DICKIE. Well—guess I'll be going.

GAYE. Don't go. You and Linda are friends, aren't you?

DICKIE. Oh, sure.

GAYE. [*Impersonally.*] She's a great girl when you really get to know her.

DICKIE. She was your secretary once, wasn't she?

GAYE. Yes—and sometimes I wish I hadn't got her in the show. She's not a bad actress, but she was the best secretary I ever had. Intelligent, accurate, thorough—and that girl could take a hundred and fifty words per minute— [LINDA *enters. Cordially.*] Hello, Linda.

LINDA. Hello, Steven. My, you're looking well! Hello, Dickie.

DICKIE. Hello, Linda.

LINDA. I hope I'm not intruding.

GAYE. Not at all. . . . Is this a social visit, or is there something special you want to see me about?

LINDA. Well . . . [*She hesitates smilingly.*] Neither.—I came to see Dickie.

DICKIE. [*Puzzled.*] See me? How did you know I was here?

LINDA. Why—uh—Flogdell told me.

GAYE. Did you hear the news about Dickie? He's leaving the show.

LINDA. Oh, really?

GAYE. Yes, isn't it too bad? He's bought a cow ranch.

LINDA. [*Cheerfully.*] Who are they going to get in his

place? I hope they get Oscar Feroni, don't you?—I think he's romantic.

GAYE. You mean that bushy-haired fellow who sprawls picturesquely on floors?

LINDA. Uh-huh. I think he plays men awfully well . . .

DICKIE. [*Awkwardly.*] Well—so long.

GAYE. What's your hurry?

LINDA. Don't go on my account. [*This is what she came in for—to clear the last vestige of suspicion from Steven's heart—and she isn't going to let DICKIE get away.*] Oh, you must tell Mr. Gaye about all the fun you had yesterday afternoon in my apartment.

DICKIE. [*Staring at her.*] Yesterday afternoon? [*Slowly.*] Oh . . . So that's where I was!—Gee, Linda, that's terrible. I—I don't quite know what to say. You see, I never drink—and yesterday I bought the ranch and—and the real estate man and I had a couple of drinks—

GAYE. A couple?

DICKIE. Exactly two—that I can remember.—Gee.—Did you have any trouble getting rid of me?

LINDA. [*Amiably.*] I don't know. I left you there. You might call on my maid and get the rest of the story.

DICKIE. Gosh.

[*The telephone rings.* GAYE *picks it up.*]

GAYE. Hello. . . . Yes. . . . All right. [*To* DICKIE.] It's Benham. Did you give him your notice?

DICKIE. An hour ago.

GAYE. He's probably calling about you. [*Into the telephone.*] Hello, Bill. . . . Yes—I know. He's here right now. . . . [*Hesitatingly.*] Well, I'll tell you.—[*He gives* DICKIE *a quick look and hesitates again.*]

DICKIE. I'll run along.

GAYE. [*To* DICKIE.] No, no, no. [*Into the telephone.*] Hold on a moment, will you, Bill? [*He puts the telephone on the table and as he goes quickly toward the bedroom—to* DICKIE.] I may want to talk to you.—I'll take it in the bedroom.

LINDA. [*Rises.*] I think I'll go, Steven. I just dropped in about the publicity for Chicago. I can see you another time.

GAYE. Please—I'll be right back. Entertain Dickie, like a nice girl.

[GAYE *goes into the bedroom.* LINDA, *for a moment functioning as a secretary, goes to the table, picks up the telephone and listens; when she is sure* GAYE *is connected, she hangs up the telephone.*]

DICKIE. [*Comes toward her.*] Listen. [LINDA *turns, startled at the sudden tension in* DICKIE'S *voice.*]

LINDA. Yes?

DICKIE. How did you know I was here?

LINDA. I didn't. I made it up when I saw you.

DICKIE. [*Steps toward her. Desperately.*] Linda! . . .

LINDA. [*A little frightened.*] What's the matter with you?

DICKIE. [*Violently.*] You.—I'm quitting the show on account of you. . . . Don't look at me like that. That's the way you've been looking at me for six months, as if I was the wallpaper on the wall. It drove me crazy.—*I remember yesterday.* I didn't buy a ranch.—I had to see you. I couldn't stand it any longer. I took a couple of drinks—I don't know how many—so I could break through that look of yours.

LINDA. Dickie—you poor boy—you poor, foolish boy. What have I done to you?

DICKIE. [*Breaking.*] Nothing. I love you so damn much I can't see straight—that's all. [*She recoils from this as if struck. He stands trembling and looking at her, defiant and afraid. Then he turns away.*]—That's all. . . .

[*Suddenly he turns and dashes out of the room. For a while* LINDA *does not move, but stands looking at the door through which* DICKIE *went. She is stirred, shaken to her toes.* GAYE *enters.*]

GAYE. Where's Dickie?

LINDA. [*Pause. She is going to lie to him for the first time— a lie of omission.*] He wanted to go, so—I didn't stop him.

GAYE. [*Settling comfortably into the sofa.*] You didn't mean what you said about Oscar Feroni, did you?

LINDA. [*Looks at him then comes over to him slowly. Intensely.*] Steven—will you marry me?

GAYE. [*Tenderly.*] Will you stick to the subject? What about Feroni?

LINDA.—Kiss me, Steven.

[*He kisses her lightly.*]

GAYE. You do love me, don't you?

LINDA. I'd like to see anybody try to stop me.

GAYE. You make me very happy.

LINDA.—Will you marry me?

GAYE.—I'm weakening.

LINDA. Oh, darling, darling—

GAYE. What are you crying about?

LINDA. Let's do it right away.

GAYE. [*Moved.*] All right. [*They kiss.*] You know I've always wanted to, don't you?

LINDA. Have you?

GAYE. I only hesitated because I wasn't really sure you loved me.—

LINDA. But now you are, aren't you?

GAYE. Somehow, I am. . . . Let's go up to Greenwich tomorrow morning.

LINDA. Done! It's a date.

[*There is a knock on the door.*]

GAYE. Yes?

[FLOGDELL *comes in.*]

FLOGDELL. It's eleven-thirty. Time to practise your piano lesson, sir.

GAYE. Thank you, Flogdell.

FLOGDELL. Not at all, sir.

[FLOGDELL *goes. The atmosphere is easy and gay.*]

GAYE. [*With an air.*] Do you realize I have mastered one of Schubert's most uncomplicated Etudes?

LINDA. Not really, Mr. Paderewski!

GAYE.—I am in the mood. I shall play for you.

LINDA. [*Goes to the desk and gets her knitting from a drawer.*] This is a moment I will cherish.

GAYE. [*Now at the piano.*] Have you ever heard a great artist play the scales?

LINDA. The scales—that's by Beethoven, isn't it?

[*He begins to play the scales a little better than badly.* LINDA *takes ash tray, her knitting and goes to the sofa.*]

GAYE. [*Continues to play.*] I can play and address remarks to my concert audience at the same time.

LINDA. [*Stretched out on sofa, smoking, knitting.*] A dual personality! . . . Steven—you're really doing it nicely. I'm proud of you.

GAYE. [*Still playing.*] What do you make of Dickie, anyway?

LINDA. [*Disturbed.*] He's a fool.

GAYE. Funny that he came to see you. [*Stops playing.*] Couldn't he remember why?

LINDA. [*Frightened—her hands petrified at their knitting.*] Apparently not.

GAYE. Funny. . . .

LINDA. [*Desperately.*] I figured he stepped out of the Waldorf Bar, walked a block, looked up and saw where I live—. What do you think?

GAYE. Well—it's hard to say. If it were in a play, I'd have a theory; but in life—well, life never makes sense. [*He turns back to the piano and continues his scales.*] Happy?

LINDA. [*Relaxing.*] Blissfully.

GAYE. [*Playing.*] You know—if I were writing a play, I'd have Dickie in love with you.

LINDA. [*Startled.*] Why?

GAYE. [*Still playing.*] It's a better reason for leaving a show than a cow ranch.—Then I'd hint to the audience either that he's not really going away, or that you like him more than you're telling. . . . [*He continues to play.*] But, thank the Lord, I'm a pianist, not a playwright. [*He continues cheerfully with his scales as*

THE CURTAIN SLOWLY FALLS

ACT TWO

Scene II

Same day. Six in the afternoon. The lamps are lit.

FLOGDELL *is drawing the window curtains. He gives the flowers on the piano a finishing touch. The telephone rings.*]

FLOGDELL. Yes? . . . Very well. . . . Good evening, Miss Linda. . . . He's dressing, Miss Linda. . . . No, the place-cards haven't come yet, but they'll be here in time. . . . Just a moment, Miss Linda. [*He takes paper and a pencil from his pocket and makes notes as he talks.*] Yes, I've got it—you at Mr. Gaye's left—Mrs. Benham at Mr. Gaye's right. Then Mr. and Mrs. Galloway. . . . Yes. . . . Of course the caterer is *supposed* to be doing the job, but I have been around all the time, keeping an eye on things. After all, even the best caterer cannot provide that additional debonair touch which we of the theatre find so necessary. . . . Yes, Miss Linda. . . . Yes. . . . [GAYE *appears at the bedroom doorway. He is in evening dress except for a houserobe.*] Here's Mr. Gaye now.

[GAYE *takes the telephone.* FLOGDELL *goes.*]

GAYE. Hello, my darling. . . . Yes, my sweet. . . . No, my darling. . . . Yes, my love. . . . Yes, my dearest. . . .

Can't you come right now? . . . Of course I want you to look beautiful, but hurry. . . . It's six now. . . . Six-thirty? Swell. That'll give us an hour and a half before the guests come.—Oh, say—does the bracelet go with the new dress? . . . Well, it's another good sign. . . . At six-thirty then. . . . By the way, I didn't ask Dickie— . . . Well, I wouldn't put it as strongly as that, but I'm glad you agree with me. . . . Au revoir, my darling, my dearest, my love. . . . What? . . . No—Greenwich is the best place. We can motor out after breakfast and be married in time for lunch. . . . Good-bye, my own! . . .

[FLOGDELL *comes in just as* GAYE *is finishing.*]

FLOGDELL. I beg your pardon, sir.

GAYE. I beg *your* pardon, Flogdell. [*He takes a flower from the vase on the piano.*]

FLOGDELL. For what, sir?

GAYE. Does it matter, Flogdell? I like you—I'm your friend —and I beg your pardon. [*He puts the flower in* FLOGDELL'S *buttonhole.*]

FLOGDELL. Thank you, sir.

GAYE. The important thing is—do you like *me*, are you *my* friend?

FLOGDELL. May I answer that by a quotation, sir?

GAYE. Please!

FLOGDELL.
   "When, to the sessions of sweet silent thought
   I summon up remembrance of things past—"

ACCENT ON YOUTH

GAYE. Flogdell!—you love me!

FLOGDELL. Have you ever doubted it for a moment, sir?

GAYE. [*Earnestly.*] Flogdell—I'm going to make an announcement at dinner tonight which will be the ultimate test of a gentleman's gentleman.

FLOGDELL. That can only mean one thing, sir.

GAYE. [*Seriously.*] I tremble for your answer.

FLOGDELL. You need not tremble, sir. . . . You see, I am —that is—I've become engaged to be married myself, sir.

GAYE. Why, Flogdell—how nice!

FLOGDELL. She's the housemaid across the street in Number Twenty-Three. It's our favorite joke, sir, that she works in Number Twenty-Three and she *is* twenty-three. If I may say so, sir, it's your play that did it.

[*They stand smiling at each other.*]

GAYE. Flogdell, do you dance?

FLOGDELL. Yes, sir.

GAYE. Will you dance with me?

FLOGDELL. Thank you, sir.

[GAYE *solemnly embraces* FLOGDELL *and, humming "The Merry Widow Waltz," they dance seven or eight steps. They are interrupted by the opening of the door. There stands* DICKIE.]

FLOGDELL. [*To* GAYE.] I beg your pardon, sir! [*Going hur-*

riedly to the door.] I had quite forgotten what I came in for. It was to tell you—that Mr. Reynolds is calling, sir.

GAYE. It was my fault, Flogdell.

FLOGDELL. Thank you, sir.

GAYE. Come in, Dickie.

[FLOGDELL *goes.* GAYE *and* DICKIE *are alone.*]

DICKIE. I—I happened to be passing—and—I thought I'd drop in to see you.

GAYE.—Something special?

DICKIE. I ran into Miss Darling today and she told me you're giving a dinner for the cast.

GAYE. Well, uh, in a way I am.

DICKIE. I haven't done anything to offend you, have I?

GAYE. No, Dickie, of course not.

DICKIE. I always thought you liked me.

GAYE. I do like you.—The only reason I didn't ask you was, after all, you're not in the cast any more. You resigned. And after the way you talked about people in the theatre, I didn't think you'd want to come.

DICKIE. [*Tensely.*] I do want to come—very much.

GAYE. That's too bad. I've invited ten people and that's all I can take care of. I'm awfully sorry.

DICKIE. Linda's going to be there, isn't she?

GAYE. [*Acutely attentive.*] Yes—why?

DICKIE. I've got to see her.

GAYE. [*Coldly.*] You know where she lives.

DICKIE. I tried to see her all afternoon; she wasn't at home to me.

GAYE. If it's about yesterday—

DICKIE. It is.

GAYE. Oh, you finally remembered!

DICKIE. [*Breaking.*] What do you mean, I finally remembered?—I *told* her.

GAYE. You told her! When?

DICKIE. Right here—when you were telephoning—I told her what it was all about. She knows.—Oh, God, Mr. Gaye, can't you see I'm in love with the girl?

GAYE. [*Stricken.*] So that's why you quit the show!

DICKIE. Sure, that's why I quit. I couldn't stand it—her acting as if I wasn't on earth—me holding her in my arms every night, and her acting as if I wasn't on earth. . . . Every time I came near her—to tell her—I couldn't.

GAYE. [*Slowly.*] But this morning, you could. . . . What did you tell her?

DICKIE. What I'm telling you.

GAYE. [*In pain.*]—You're sure she understood what you were saying?

DICKIE. She heard me, all right.

ACCENT ON YOUTH

GAYE. . . . What did she say?

DICKIE. I didn't wait to find out. I lost my nerve. I—I bolted.

GAYE. Why didn't you stay? [*Savagely.*] You damn fool, she'd have jumped into your arms.

DICKIE. Oh, gee—do you really think so!—No, you're wrong.—What's the matter with me, Mr. Gaye? You know me. You're a man of the world—you've lived—you're old enough to be my father. Tell me what's the matter with me.

GAYE. [*Bitterly.*] Nothing's the matter with you. You've got everything. Youth—and everything. . . . If you want her, go after her.

DICKIE. If it were any other girl—I never had trouble like this before—but she's different.—You know her, Mr. Gaye. You've known her a long time. She thinks all the world of you—anyone can see that. She looks up to you.—You've been in love yourself, haven't you?

GAYE. Well—go on. What do you want?

DICKIE. Understanding. I don't know whom to turn to.—Let me come tonight. I'll shoot the works the first chance I get. I've got to have my break with her. I never really had it. Every man has a right to have one break, anyway, if he's in love with a woman.—You're a man and I'm a man—and she doesn't mean anything to you— Or does she?

GAYE. [*Slowly.*] Not a damn thing.

DICKIE. Then will you help me?

GAYE. Help you? Hell, I'll give her to you. You want your break—well, I'll hand it to you on a silver platter. She's due here at six-thirty—you know, ex-secretary helping with the place-cards.—Well, I'll be gone, and she'll find you— [*Turning away quickly and going to the bedroom door.*] —The guests don't arrive until eight. That gives you an hour and a half. . . . You should be able to—get your message over in an hour and a half, don't you think?

DICKIE. I—I'll try.

GAYE. [*At the door.*] Well—the stage is yours.

[GAYE *goes.* DICKIE *stands, somewhat dazed by the abruptness of* GAYE's *departure. He looks at his watch. Then he pulls himself together and begins to pace the room, impatient for and yet afraid of the moment when* LINDA *will come. The next moment* GAYE *re-enters through the Center door. He's in tails and top hat and carries his dress overcoat and stick.*]

GAYE. If she wants to know what happened to me, tell her —tell her I got a great idea for a play and went down to the river to think it over.—There's the bell. The butler'll get you anything you want—anything at all. [*He starts out.*]

DICKIE. Mr. Gaye—[GAYE *turns.*] How will I—what'll I say to her?

GAYE. What'll you say to her!

DICKIE. I—gosh, I don't know how to begin.

GAYE. This is marvelous! . . . What do you expect me to do—write your love scene for you, too!

DICKIE. That's not what I mean. Naturally not. That would be ridiculous.

GAYE. Well, what *do* you mean?

DICKIE. I don't know what I mean. I guess it's just that I wish I had your brains.

GAYE. My brains and your body, eh?

DICKIE. Well, a fellow can wish, can't he? . . . Take the lines you wrote for me in the show. [*Half to himself.*]— Wouldn't it be wonderful if I—just for an hour—when I'm alone with her—. You see, I've got the feelings and the thoughts, but I—I never seem to find the words.

GAYE. Well, Romeo, you're all out of luck. . . . Good-bye.

DICKIE. [*Resignedly.*] Okay, Mr. Gaye.

[GAYE *puts his hand on the door-knob and then turns, fascinated in spite of himself.*]

GAYE. You've been in the show with her for six months, and three weeks of rehearsal. Didn't you ever talk to her?

DICKIE. Sure I did—at first, when she—before it happened. But afterwards—I couldn't find a tongue in my head.

GAYE. [*Comes into the room, hat on.*] What did you say to her this morning?

DICKIE. I don't remember.

GAYE. Well, for instance, did you say those classic words, "I love you?"

DICKIE. I said, "I love you so damn much I can't see straight."

GAYE. Not bad . . . !

DICKIE. [*Eagerly.*] Honestly?

GAYE.—What did she say?

DICKIE. She said—

GAYE. Never mind—don't tell me. . . .

DICKIE. Do you think, if I said the same thing to her—

GAYE. No. That's only good the first time.

DICKIE. . . . I guess you're right.

[*Pause.*]

GAYE. This thing is getting me. . . . [*Slowly.*] I could write that scene for you so that you couldn't miss—if in her heart she really cares a damn about you.

DICKIE. Gee, Mr. Gaye—would you?

GAYE. [*Awed at himself. Scarcely aware of* DICKIE.] Nothing like it has ever been done before—of course, there was Cyrano, but this is different. . . . Let's see.—[*Completely the artist now.*] . . . You're sitting here. [*He indicates a chair with his walking stick.*] The door opens. She comes in. At first, she doesn't see you.—What's the matter with me, am I going insane? The hell with you!

DICKIE. Mr. Gaye—if you've really got an idea, you *must* help me. I know writing is your profession—and if it's money, my father left me fifteen hundred shares of American Tel and Tel.—

GAYE. [*Half to himself.*] Don't interrupt me. . . . I'd be the sap of the world to do it—and yet I can't walk out on it. . . . If Molnar were in a spot like this, he'd go through with it. . . . So would Sheridan. . . . [*He stops short and turns to* DICKIE, *who is watching him in suspense. He puts his coat on a chair and his stick on the desk.*] Well, Dickie—you win. Let's shoot the works.—We'll *all* of us shoot the works. . . . Now look—

DICKIE. [*Helpfully going to the chair* GAYE *had indicated.*] I'm sitting here.

GAYE. Doesn't matter where you sit.—She comes in. You tell her, as simply as you can, that you're leaving for Europe tonight on—fake it—say the *Ile de France.* Tell her you're all packed. [*Slowly.*] You're going because of her. Whether she likes it or not, she has changed your whole life. She has made life more beautiful, more exciting, more painful. Be sure to get that in.

DICKIE. [*Repeats.*] More beautiful, more exciting, more painful.

GAYE. Right.—There's nothing as dull as just "I love you." —Now, this is a good-bye scene. That's what makes it strong. You're going away forever. You're never going to see her again—you're never going to see this country again —all because of her. *She's* never going to see *you* again. . . .

DICKIE. Say, that's swell—she may even think I'm going to kill myself!

GAYE. No, no! No suicide. No hint of suicide. That's unfair
—to all parties concerned.

DICKIE. Okay.

GAYE. Now. Carry that good-bye scene right to the door.
—She'll come to you. Start out of the door. Then turn. Ask
her to kiss you good-bye.—Think you can do that?

DICKIE. I know I can.

GAYE. All right. . . . The rest is up to you.

DICKIE. . . . Suppose she won't kiss me?

GAYE. She will. It's a good-bye scene. Any woman would.
And after that it's up to the actors, not the playwright. The
emotion is there, the moment has been created—and your
bodies are there. . . . You'll find out all you need to know
—we'll all find out.

DICKIE. Mr. Gaye. . . . Gee—you're brilliant.

GAYE. Maybe I am—[*Slowly.*] and maybe I'm not.

[GAYE *takes his coat and walks out. Now* DICKIE *is alone.
He looks at his watch. He moves impatiently about the
room. He pushes the bell. In a moment* FLOGDELL *enters.*]

FLOGDELL. Did you ring, sir?

DICKIE. Yes. [*He looks at his watch again.*] I've got twenty
after six. What time have you got?

FLOGDELL. Nineteen and a half, sir.

DICKIE. Thank you.

FLOGDELL. [*Straightening an ash tray.*]—Did Mr. Gaye say where he was going, sir?

DICKIE. No, he didn't.

FLOGDELL. Thank you, sir. . . . I understand you're not going to Chicago with the play, sir.

DICKIE. No, I'm not.

FLOGDELL. [*Fixing another ash tray.*] If I may say so, it will be a great loss, sir. I agree with the phrasing of the critic in Variety who said: "The boy's got something."

DICKIE. Very nice of you—thank you.

FLOGDELL. [*In the doorway.*] In fact, as I said to my future wife—what a Romeo Mr. Reynolds would make!

[DICKIE, *staggered, stares as* FLOGDELL *goes.* DICKIE *moves about restlessly for a few moments and then sits down before the piano. Aimlessly, with one finger, he begins to play.* LINDA *comes bursting in.*]

LINDA. Steven! [*She sees it is* DICKIE.] Oh. [DICKIE *rises, confused—and overawed by the stunning effect of* LINDA *in her new evening dress.*] Where's Mr. Gaye?

DICKIE. He went out. [*He takes a deep breath.*] He said—

LINDA. When'll he be back?

DICKIE.—Not for an hour and a half.

LINDA. What are you doing here?

DICKIE. I—I came—

LINDA. You're not invited to the party tonight, are you?

DICKIE. I—I don't know.

LINDA. Well, if you are, I won't come.

DICKIE. Linda, will you listen to me—

LINDA. No. I don't want to hear a word you have to say. I don't want to see you. I don't want to be in the same room with you. Either you go, or I go.

[*Pause.*]

DICKIE. [*Licked.*]—I'll go. [*He moves slowly toward the door. Getting set.*] But before I go, I want to tell you—

LINDA. And go as far away as you possibly can. Nothing would please me better than to know you were in China, or Europe or New Zealand—

DICKIE. [*Violently.*] All right!

LINDA.—Or anywhere where you couldn't pester me on the telephone.

DICKIE. [*Comes over to her swiftly.*] Shut up! [*He grabs her roughly by the shoulders.*] Now listen to me!

[LINDA *looks at him a little breathlessly. He realizes he has nothing to say, and swept by the impetus of his own movement, he suddenly takes her in his arms and kisses her.* LINDA *fights him off.* DICKIE *relaxes his hold but doesn't let her go.*]

LINDA. [*Trying to push him away and pounding at him—in a low, frantic tone.*] Let me go! Let me go, I tell you!

DICKIE. I love you.

LINDA. What's the matter with you—are you crazy?

DICKIE. [*Still holding her.*] I love you.

LINDA. I hate you—oh, how I hate you!

DICKIE. [*Over her words.*] I love you, I love you, I love you, I love you, I love you, I love you, I—

[*He kisses her again. She tries violently to resist, but he holds her close. Gradually her resistance breaks down, and soon she is limp in his arms. After a while, he releases her. They stand, shaken, looking at each other with new eyes. Then they go into each other's arms again, and now LINDA is kissing as well as being kissed. In the middle of this kiss, unseen by LINDA or DICKIE, the door opens and GAYE enters, still wearing his hat and carrying his top-coat. He stands arrested by the sight of the embracing couple. The kiss lasts another few moments. Then LINDA draws slowly away from DICKIE. DICKIE sees GAYE first. LINDA follows DICKIE'S look. She is paralyzed at the sight of GAYE.*]

GAYE. Excuse me. [*He goes a few steps to the desk.*] I came for my walking stick. [*He picks up the stick, tucks it under his arm and moves to the door.*] . . . You may not know it—but that was a curtain line.

[*He goes. The two stand looking at the door through which GAYE went.*]

CURTAIN

ACT THREE

ACT THREE

The following October. Evening.

The piano has disappeared, LINDA'S *photograph and lampshade are gone, and the room has the original bachelor's careless arrangement of furniture.*

We discover GAYE *and* GALLOWAY *deeply studying a checkerboard. They are seated at a small table.* GAYE *is in a velvet smoking jacket. He looks older—this is accentuated by spectacles.* FLOGDELL *is mixing whisky and soda. As the two sit in silence,* FLOGDELL *pours two drinks and sets one by each. Then he goes back quietly, sits down in the chair opposite* GALLOWAY, *and we realize by his behavior that he is the one who is playing with* GALLOWAY, GAYE *being the onlooker.*

FLOGDELL. Have you moved, sir?

GALLOWAY. [*Indicating his move.*] Yes—I jumped you.

FLOGDELL. Well! . . . I'm sorry, sir, but I shall have to jump you three—[*He does.*] and that gives me another king.

GALLOWAY. Oh, my!—I didn't see that, did you, Steven?

GAYE. My dear Frank, I saw it coming ten minutes ago.

ACCENT ON YOUTH

GALLOWAY. Well, I haven't noticed *you* winning any games from Flogdell.

FLOGDELL. It is my observation that artists are never good checker players, sir.

GAYE.—Jump him, Frank—you've got to.

GALLOWAY. Where? . . . [*In dismay.*] Oh, oh, oh! [*In distress he makes the move, and* FLOGDELL *thereupon cleans up the rest of* GALLOWAY'S *men.*]

GAYE. That's game.

FLOGDELL. Sorry, Mr. Galloway.

GAYE. Come on—give Flogdell his quarter.

GALLOWAY. [*As he pays* FLOGDELL *his winnings.*] I don't mind losing, Steven, but you constantly distract me with your asides.

GAYE. And what about your humming and drumming with your knuckles—do you call that checker-manners? I challenge you to a game without sound effects.

GALLOWAY. No, thank you. I've got to get home. [*He rises.*] If I'm not home by ten-thirty, Roberta worries.

GAYE. [*Coaxingly.*] One more drink. It's lonely here without you—isn't it, Flogdell?

[FLOGDELL, *who is replenishing the glasses, bows acquiescence.*]

GALLOWAY. Very well. Just soda for me. No Scotch.

GAYE. Have a night-cap with us, Flogdell.

FLOGDELL. [*Raises his scarcely touched first drink.*] Thank
you, sir. [*He serves* GALLOWAY.]

[GAYE *waves* FLOGDELL *into a chair. Now the three men are
comfortably seated, glasses in hand.*]

FLOGDELL. By the way, Mr. Galloway, Mrs. Flogdell tried
that recipe of Mrs. Galloway's and I must report that for
lightness, delicacy of flavor, and sheer melting delicious-
ness, we have never tasted such biscuits.

GALLOWAY. I'm charmed. And how is the little woman?

FLOGDELL. Doing very nicely, sir—very.

GALLOWAY. Don't forget to let us know when the time
comes, will you?

FLOGDELL. You may count on me to advise you of the im-
pending arrival of young Steven Galloway Flogdell.

GAYE. Here's to him.

[*They all drink.*]

GAYE. [*To* GALLOWAY.] How are your Memoirs progress-
ing, Frank?

GALLOWAY. Splendidly. I'm just past my childhood. I had
a particularly unhappy childhood.

GAYE. Who hasn't?

FLOGDELL. If I may say so, sir, *my* childhood memories are
among my sweetest ones.

GALLOWAY. —There was one boy I couldn't lick, and it embittered my life up to the age of fifteen. The last I heard of him, he was driving a truck.

GAYE. There wasn't a boy on my street who couldn't lick me. . . .

FLOGDELL. . . . I was very handy with my fists as a youngster. I seriously considered a career in the professional ring.

GAYE *and* GALLOWAY. [*Leaning forward.*] Really!

FLOGDELL. I have always believed in the culture of the body as well as the mind. I'm into my sixties, but—[*He rises.*] if you will permit me, I can still touch the floor with my fists.

GAYE. Please, Flogdell!

[FLOGDELL *tries and doesn't quite make it.*]

FLOGDELL. [*Flustered.*] I do it every morning in my pajamas! If I may remove my coat, sir—

GAYE. Please!

[FLOGDELL *does, and this time he touches the floor successfully.*]

GAYE. Marvelous!

GALLOWAY. [*Patronizingly.*] Nice. Uh—nice.

GAYE. Can *you* do it?

[GALLOWAY *stands up, takes off his coat, and without a word duplicates* FLOGDELL'S *performance.*]

ACCENT ON YOUTH

FLOGDELL. I salute you, sir.—Pardon me, sir, but may I feel your muscles?

GALLOWAY. With pleasure. [FLOGDELL *feels his bicep.*] Go ahead—feel me all over.

FLOGDELL. [*Feels* GALLOWAY's *biceps, shoulders and thighs.*] You're a fine physical specimen, sir. . . . You may, me— if you wish, sir.

GALLOWAY. Thank you. [*He performs the same ritual with* FLOGDELL. [*Admiringly.*] Hard as nails.

FLOGDELL. Thank you, sir.

GALLOWAY. Do you know anything about Indian wrestling?

FLOGDELL. [*Puzzled.*] Indian wrestling?

GALLOWAY. [*Smugly.*] I'll show you how it's done. [*Demonstrating.*] You put your foot here—stand like this—give me your hand—the point is to see which man can unbalance the other. . . .

FLOGDELL. [*Leaning forward and unbalancing* GALLOWAY.] You mean like this, sir?

[GALLOWAY *lands sprawling on the floor,* FLOGDELL *still holding his hand.*]

GALLOWAY. [*On the floor.*] Yes, that's what I meant!

FLOGDELL [*Helping him up.*]— I *beg* your pardon, sir.

[*Both, back to back, put on their coats.*]

GAYE. Flogdell—

FLOGDELL. [*The servant again.*] Yes, sir.

GAYE. Pour me another drink.

FLOGDELL. Very well, sir.

GALLOWAY. [*Collecting himself.*] And, ah, I'll have one, too.

FLOGDELL. Yes, sir.

GALLOWAY.—With just a tiny bit of Scotch in it.

FLOGDELL. Very well, sir.

[*As FLOGDELL prepares the drinks:*]

GALLOWAY. [*Sitting.*] You know, I miss "Old Love."

GAYE. I'm glad it's over.

GALLOWAY. That play affected my life. . . . It did something to all of us. Linda marrying Dickie; Miss Darling getting a Hollywood contract. . . . I thought either it would be a smash hit, like a Eugene O'Neill play, or a dreadful failure, like—like a Eugene O'Neill play. But who would have predicted that it would turn out just a show.

GAYE. You're depressing me.

GALLOWAY. [*Hastily.*] Oh, it was a splendid piece of work —but I do think your next should be a comedy.

GAYE. I haven't got a next. . . .

GALLOWAY. —What's the matter with you, anyway, Steven?

GAYE. Nothing. I'm getting old, that's all.

GALLOWAY. Well, so am I.

GAYE. You *are* old.

GALLOWAY. You say it as if it were a crime, instead of a pleasure.

GAYE. You *like* it, do you?

[*Pause.*]

GALLOWAY.—Steven, you ought to go out more—see people—why, you know half New York. After all, at your age a man should begin to enjoy life—travel, see new countries—

GAYE. I've been thinking about it, Frank. . . . But every time I sit down with a map and a travel folder, I realize there's no trip as beautiful as Act One of a new play.

[FLOGDELL, *who has left the room some time during the above scene, now enters.*]

FLOGDELL. Miss Genevieve Lang calling, sir.

GAYE. [*Surprised.*] Genevieve Lang!

FLOGDELL. She says she wishes to see you only for a moment, sir.

GAYE. . . . All right—show her up.

[FLOGDELL *has almost reached the door when he turns.*]

FLOGDELL. [*To* GALLOWAY.] Pardon me, sir, I promised Mrs. Galloway that you'd make your exit by ten-fifteen.

GALLOWAY. [*Rising.*] Oh, yes, yes, yes—thank you, Flogdell.—Good-bye, Steven. [*He is about to follow* FLOGDELL, *then impulsively he turns and goes over to* GAYE, *puts his hand on* GAYE's *shoulder.*] Steven—think over what I said. You're alone too much. You ought to bring youth into your life. I may say that I'm glad a young lady is visiting you, and furthermore I may say—

GAYE. [*Interrupting and patting his cheeks.*] He said exit, not exit speech.

GALLOWAY. [*Hurt, with dignity.*]—As I was saying, good night, Steven.

GAYE. Good night, Frank.

[*They shake hands.* GALLOWAY *goes to the door, still retaining his dignity.* FLOGDELL *holds the door for him. As he reaches the door, he puts his arm around* FLOGDELL's *shoulder and the two go out together.* GAYE *stands quietly for a moment, then he goes to a small wall mirror, runs his hand through his hair to smooth it. He takes off his glasses and looks at himself. He decides not to wear his glasses. He picks up his spectacle-case from the table, is about to put the glasses away and then changes his mind, puts the glasses on again. The next moment* GENEVIEVE *enters. She is in evening clothes.*]

GENEVIEVE. Steven!

GAYE. Genevieve!

GENEVIEVE. You must forgive my rushing in like this—but I was at the opera and in the first intermission I glanced at my program and what do I see—the date: October ninth. I flew out, bought some flowers, jumped into a taxi, and here I am! [GAYE *stares at her. She smiles back, enjoying his confusion.* FLOGDELL *enters, carrying a vase with red flowers.*] Thank you, Flogdell. Set them down—let me see —this desk would be nice.

[FLOGDELL *obeys and goes.*]

GAYE. [*Puzzled.*] They're beautiful, Genevieve—thank you. But—

GENEVIEVE. But what? [*Studying him with a smile.*] I suppose the ninth of October doesn't mean a thing to you.

GAYE. It was the day—ah—wasn't it the day when—[*He hesitates.*]

GENEVIEVE. It was—and it was the luckiest day of my life. Do you know what happened to me?

GAYE. I've often wondered.

GENEVIEVE. I went to Finland!

GAYE. Did you!

GENEVIEVE. I did!—Steven, the Finns are the most wonderful people in the world. I brought one back with me. We just arrived last week.—I've been on the verge of calling you a thousand times, but you know what a dither one gets into when one is buying a trousseau.—What a year, what a year! Keep next Monday free—you're coming to my wedding.

GAYE. With pleasure, my dear child.

GENEVIEVE. And now—good-bye. Knut will wonder what's become of me, and he has a Finnish temper—pun.

GAYE. [*Accompanying her to the door.*] What's Knut like, young or rich?

GENEVIEVE. Nobody's poor in Finland,—and he's exactly my age, but he doesn't know it.

GAYE. Genevieve, you haven't changed a bit.

GENEVIEVE. Oh yes, I have—completely. It's my favorite subject. Don't ask me how, or I'll spend the evening telling you.

GAYE. How?

GENEVIEVE. I'm in love. Try it yourself some time.

GAYE. I have, thank you.

GENEVIEVE. You mean—love?

GAYE. [*Spelling it.*] L-o-v-e.

GENEVIEVE. . . . You don't look very happy.

GAYE.—I lost.

[*She studies him a moment in silence, then she goes down to a chair and sits. As she lights a cigarette:*]

GENEVIEVE. Knut can wait. It'll do him good.—Tell me about it. . . . When did you meet her?

GAYE. . . . October the ninth.

GENEVIEVE. Oh!—how interesting!— . . . Do I know her?

GAYE. [*Wearily.*] What's the difference?

[*Pause.*]

GENEVIEVE. How's the work?

GAYE. There isn't any. . . .

GENEVIEVE. Now, Steven, love is the greatest thing on earth and all that—but don't be a baby.

GAYE. I'm not. I'm an old man.

[*Pause.*]

GENEVIEVE. Somehow I can't imagine you losing a girl if you really wanted to hold her.

GAYE. [*Savagely.*] I *gave* her away! Why, he wouldn't have had a chance. But I saw something between them—*he* didn't know it was there—and I, *I* wrote his love scene, *I* staged it, *I* gave him the setting—*I put the words into his mouth.* . . . Well, I did a good job.—And now they're happily married.

GENEVIEVE. Do you think that was very bright?

GAYE. There's no fool like an old playwright. . . . Genevieve, Genevieve, I always thought when you got older, you got wiser. Well, it doesn't help. You know what it's all about, but don't let anybody tell you that lessens the pain.

GENEVIEVE. —Steven, why don't you travel? Look what it's done for me! . . . See new places, new faces—get out in the open air—play golf.

GAYE. [*Patiently.*] Listen, Genevieve—I don't like golf.

GENEVIEVE. I'll tell you what—join us at the opera, and then we'll all go somewhere.

GAYE. I don't like opera.

GENEVIEVE. Well—there's only one thing left for you to do.

ACCENT ON YOUTH

GAYE. I don't like suicide!

[*Suddenly they both look up. The door has swept open and there is* LINDA, *carrying a huge bouquet of yellow flowers. She is wearing a sports coat over a dinner gown. She stops short at the sight of* GENEVIEVE. GAYE *has risen. Pause.*]

LINDA. Hello!

GAYE. [*After getting his breath.*] Good evening. [*Pause.*] Do you ladies know each other? Miss Lang, Miss Brown— I mean Mrs. Reynolds.

GENEVIEVE. How do you do.

LINDA. How do you do. [*Pause.*] I suppose you don't know what day today is.

GAYE. [*Maliciously.*] Tuesday?

LINDA. It's October the ninth.

GAYE. So it is.

LINDA. I brought you some flowers.

GAYE. So I see.

GENEVIEVE. [*Being nice.*] Aren't they lovely!

LINDA. [*Looking around.*] Where can I put them? [GAYE *goes to the bell.*] Never mind. [*Going to the vase containing* GENEVIEVE's *flowers.*] We can throw these out. They don't look so good. [*She puts her flowers on the table, takes* GENEVIEVE's *flowers from the vase and puts them into the wastebasket. Then, while* GAYE *and* GENEVIEVE *exchange dazed glances, she puts her own flowers into the vase.*] I

ACCENT ON YOUTH

think yellow goes better in this room. There! [*She looks defiantly at the other two. Pause.*]

GENEVIEVE. Well! . . . [*She goes over to the wastebasket containing her flowers, which happen to have fallen right ends up. She picks up the wastebasket as if it were a vase and marches to the still open door.*] Good-bye! [*She goes. There is a moment's silence.*]

LINDA. Were those her flowers?

GAYE. They were, but the wastebasket is mine.

LINDA. What is she to you?

GAYE. Say—how did you get in here, anyway—and what do you want?

LINDA. You've got to answer my question, Steven—what is she to you?

GAYE.—A friend.

LINDA. What do you mean, a friend?

GAYE. A girl I never was in love with.

[*Pause.*]

LINDA. Steven, will you take me back?

GAYE. Is that how little you know me?

LINDA. [*Taking off her coat.*] You've got to take me back. You don't know what I've been through. I've been in hell for five months. No matter what I've done to you, I've paid for it. I lead a life of torture—it's become a nightmare— you're the only one who can save me.

ACCENT ON YOUTH

GAYE. Don't you love him any more?

LINDA. I can't stand him!

GAYE. You loved him—when you married him . . . didn't you?

LINDA.—I thought I did. It all happened so quickly, how could I tell? I married him that same night—I left the show —you were so mean about everything, I hated you. . . . I could have loved him; I wanted to; I tried.—And then came the honeymoon. . . . I never want to go through anything like it again. Oh, Steven, why didn't you tell me what a dreadful thing youth was—why didn't anybody tell me! —We went to Santa Barbara. Here's a typical honeymoon day: out of bed at seven—A. M. not P. M.—three hasty kisses, a shower, then we play tennis—what do I know about tennis? Then, sweating and limp, another shower, two hasty kisses, and swimming, while I sit on the beach and burn. —Did you ever see the rich men's sons in their bathing suits waiting for the depression to pass? They're broad-shouldered, handsome, tan—every one of them was once an All-American something—and ten feet away you can't tell one from the other . . . and you couldn't tell Dickie from any of them.—Then he gets a rub-down and it's time for lunch. Oh, Steven, after sitting with a clean-cut outdoors man and watching him eat vitamins, starches and spinach, you and your pills are a Midsummer Night's Dream.—Going to bed with him was just like going to bed with the front page of a physical culture magazine: in the first place, I was too exhausted by that time to care for him even if I hadn't begun to hate him; and there you lie, unable to sleep because the lights are on—and why are the lights on? Because Lionel

Strongfort has to do his setting-up exercises: it seems that somewhere during the day he missed out on a couple of muscles.—Then a home in Connecticut, fox-hunting, golf, polo. . . . Five months of it, Steven—five months without night life, without the theatre, without glasses of beer pounding the table because somebody has got something crazy and beautiful and passionate to say to somebody else, without cigarettes and poetry and laughter and bad ventilation, without dialogue—without you, Steven. . . .

GAYE. Where's Dickie?

LINDA. He's at the Waldorf.

GAYE. Does he know you're here?

LINDA. No.

GAYE. Where does he think you are?

LINDA. I don't know. I left him a note telling him good-bye and that I wanted a divorce.

GAYE.—Does he still love you?

LINDA. What do you think?

GAYE. I think he does—and I think you should go back to him. . . .

LINDA. Don't you care for me any more?

GAYE. No.

LINDA. I love you more than ever. I know I've hurt you, Steven, frightfully—but I'll make it up to you. It's October the ninth—our anniversary—I had to come back to you.

It's been a wonderful and terrible year for both of us. We're ready for each other now.

GAYE. [*Slowly.*] I would like it very much if I never saw you any more, or heard from you—or anything.

[*There is a silence while she looks at him and realizes fully what he's been through.*]

LINDA. Steven, I'm never going to make the mistake of leaving you again.

[*There is a pause. Then* GAYE *gets up and goes to the telephone. He dials it.*]

GAYE. [*Into the telephone.*] Waldorf-Astoria? . . . Mr. Richard Reynolds, please.

LINDA. What are you going to do?

GAYE. I'm going to have your husband come and get you. [LINDA *thinks this over for a second, then lights a cigarette and settles back in her chair. Into the telephone.*] Are you sure he doesn't? . . . Will you ring him again, please. [*There is a knock at the door.*] Come in. [FLOGDELL *enters, somewhat agitated.*] What is it, Flogdell?

FLOGDELL. It's Mr. Reynolds, sir.

[GAYE *hangs up the telephone.*]

GAYE.—Send him up.

FLOGDELL. I beg your pardon, sir—but he's not precisely in the apartment. [*Looking for a moment at* LINDA *and then back to* GAYE.] He has two other gentlemen with him, sir

—and a detective. He seems to be in quite a state, and I thought it best not to admit him until I had consulted with you.

GAYE. Does he know Miss Linda is here?

FLOGDELL. I took it upon myself to say she was not here, sir—but the detective contradicted me through the aperture.

[GAYE *looks at* LINDA. *She is sitting erect and looking back at him a little breathlessly, but she doesn't say a word.* GAYE *turns to* FLOGDELL.]

GAYE.—Let them come up.

FLOGDELL.—Including the detective, sir?

GAYE. No—you may exclude the detective, Flogdell.

FLOGDELL. Very well, sir.

[*He goes.* GAYE *stands a moment in thought.* LINDA *hasn't moved, nor has she once taken her eyes off him. Now* GAYE *goes to the bedroom door and holds it open.*]

GAYE. Get in there. [*She hesitates an instant, then takes her coat and goes in. He goes to the door and makes sure it is shut. Then he goes quickly to the bookshelves, takes a book, and sits down. The next moment* FLOGDELL *opens the door, and* DICKIE *enters, followed by two young men who are cut from the same pattern as* DICKIE—*tanned, broad-shouldered, well-tailored college men.* GAYE *rises with a very cordial smile.* FLOGDELL *stays.*] Why, hello, Dickie! How are you? It's about time you came to see me! Where's Linda?

DICKIE. [*Ignoring* GAYE'S *outstretched hand. Grimly.*] You know damn well where she is.

GAYE. [*Looking bewildered.*] Do I?

DICKIE. She's right here, in this apartment.

GAYE. Linda?

DICKIE. Yes, Linda.

GAYE. Flogdell, has Mrs. Reynolds been here this evening?

FLOGDELL. No, sir.

DICKIE. Be careful what you say. You're in the presence of witnesses.

GAYE. [*Annoyed.*] Look here—I don't recall inviting you or these splendid physical specimens to my apartment.

FLOGDELL. Pardon me, sir, but if you have changed your mind about seeing these gentlemen, it would be a pleasure to show them out, sir.

FIRST FRIEND. [*Aggressively.*] You and who else?

FLOGDELL. Just I, sir.

GAYE. Thank you very much, Flogdell—but I'm afraid you might lose your temper. You may go.

FLOGDELL.—Very well, sir. [*He goes.*]

DICKIE. Now, fellows, before we search the house, look around—and remember everything you see. [*He holds* GAYE'S *eye challengingly as:*]

FIRST FRIEND. Two high-balls. one empty.

SECOND FRIEND. Three cigarettes, no lip rouge marks—

FIRST FRIEND. One checkerboard—

SECOND FRIEND. [*Picking it up.*] One hairpin.

DICKIE. [*Starting for the bedroom door.*] All right—let's go.

GAYE. [*Steps in front of him.*] Before you make another move, I wish to call your attention to the fact that you're in the United States of America, not Princeton.

[*Pause.*]

DICKIE. —One hour ago Linda slipped out of the hotel. She left this note.

[*He hands* GAYE *the note.* GAYE *reads it.*]

GAYE. [*With an air of astonishment.*] My goodness gracious!

DICKIE. [*Takes back the note.*] You were the first one I suspected.

GAYE. *Me?*

DICKIE. Yes, you. For five months all I've heard, morning, noon, and night, is Steven Gaye. Like a fool, I was broad-minded. I was dumb enough to believe there's one gentleman in the lousy world of the theatre. Well—I know better now.

GAYE. Just what is it that you know now?

DICKIE. [*With deliberation.*] My wife, carrying a bouquet of flowers, walked around this block five times—and then she entered your house.—Well, if you two think you can make a fool of me, you're mistaken. I live in a respectable community, I've got a position to maintain—and if anybody gets the divorce, *I* get it.

GAYE. Dickie, will you be good enough to dismiss the glee club, and sit down, and tell me what this is all about?

DICKIE.—And if she thinks she's going to get any alimony, she's got another—

[DICKIE *stops cold for the bedroom door opens and* LINDA, *very cool and casual, but frightened and unhappy underneath, strolls in. She has taken off her dress and her shoes. Over her slip she wears an old bathrobe of* GAYE'S *and on her feet she wears a pair of* GAYE'S *bedroom slippers.*]

LINDA. [*As she enters.*] Steven—where are the cigarettes? —Oh, hello, Dickie. And Butch!

FIRST FRIEND. [*Offended.*] I'm not Butch.

LINDA. [*Amiably.*] I'm sorry. I always get you boys mixed. You're Chuck, aren't you—and *he's* Butch.

DICKIE. Just what I expected to find! *Fellows, I want you to remember every word that's being said in this room.*

[*The three young men stand like military guards. Pause.*]

GAYE. [*To* LINDA.] Uh—won't you sit down?

LINDA. [*Picking up the bathrobe skirt with sixteenth century elegance and going to the sofa.*] With pleasure.

GAYE. You wanted a cigarette, didn't you?

LINDA. Please.

[*He gives her one with an elaborately gallant gesture.*]

GAYE. Light?

LINDA. Thank you.

[GAYE *lights one for himself and lounges gracefully on the sofa, ignoring the three young men, who remain standing.*]

GAYE. Have you read any good books lately?

LINDA. Well—yes and no.

GAYE. Lovely weather we're having.

LINDA. [*Coyly.*] I wouldn't put it past you.

[*Pause.*]

GAYE. [*Indicating his old bathrobe she is wearing.*] What a beautiful garment! I've been admiring it all evening.

LINDA. Yes, it's a little model by Patou. Patou took one look at me and he said, "Girlie, I got just the thing for you!"

[FLOGDELL, *without knocking, enters. He has taken this upon himself—just to be sure his master is safe.*]

FLOGDELL. Did you ring, sir?

GAYE. [*Who hasn't been near the bell.*] Why—er—yes, Flogdell!

LINDA. Where's the champagne?

FLOGDELL. The champagne?

GAYE. *The* champagne!

FLOGDELL. Oh, yes, sir. How many glasses, sir?

ACCENT ON YOUTH

GAYE. Flogdell, don't be stupid. There are only two of us.

FLOGDELL. [*Looking from* GAYE *to* LINDA, *from* LINDA *to* GAYE *and then from the two of them to the three silent young men. To* GAYE.] What happened to the three gentlemen who were here, sir?

[*Pause.*]

DICKIE. All right, fellows. [*Flanked by the two young men, he marches over to* GAYE *and* LINDA. *Like a lawyer:*] Do you fellows know this woman?

FRIENDS. We do.

DICKIE. Is she or is she not my wife?

FRIENDS. She is.

DICKIE. Please observe in detail the nature of her attire.

[LINDA *shrinks a little at this and draws the hitherto open bathrobe closely about her.*]

FRIENDS. Okay. Right.

DICKIE. We'll see who's going to get the divorce. [*He starts for the door. Turning to* GAYE.] And you——. Thought you were smart, didn't you! Deliberately giving me a love lesson—teaching me how to win her—passing your ex-mistress off on me! Well, your lesson wasn't so hot. She was so glad to get a husband, she just fell into my arms and I didn't have to say a word except I love you.

[*He walks out, followed by the other two.* LINDA *and* GAYE *sit stricken. The crudeness of* DICKIE'S *attack has stripped them of all gaiety.* FLOGDELL *hesitates a moment after the*

ACCENT ON YOUTH

*three have passed through the door, and then, seeing he is
not wanted, he follows them, shutting the door carefully behind him.* LINDA *and* GAYE *sit speechless for a moment, and
then* LINDA *suddenly begins to weep.* GAYE *stands looking
after the departed ones.*]

LINDA. [*Quietly.*] Steven.

[*He turns.*]

GAYE. Yes—?

LINDA. When I came in, I thought I wanted you—and I
thought you would *have* to want me if I wanted you. I
thought to myself, as I was walking around and around and
around the block, In another five years he'll be almost sixty
and interested in bigger things than love, and I'll be thirty
which nowadays is very young, and then we'll really be
through with each other, and by that time somebody else
will probably fall in love with me whom I'll be able to en-
dure, because although I'm not a Garbo people do seem to
be falling in love with me recently—there were two up in
Connecticut—. You see, Steven, I've become quite mature
and realistic, don't you think, and not the romantic girl who
once thought life was a flame just because you lived and
breathed, and to tell the truth I even thought so when I was
walking around the block—but you must agree I'm being
sensible now.

GAYE. [*Absently.*] You are, Linda. Very sensible.

LINDA. And I *have* changed, haven't I?

GAYE. Yes—you have.

❧ III ❧

ACCENT ON YOUTH

LINDA. And knowing you as well as I do—well, after all,
you've had your affairs, you've been married even, and I'm
sure in each case you thought this is the one great love, this
is the mountain top, this is the glory that will never end,
just as you did with me. . . . Didn't you? [GAYE *doesn't
answer; he hasn't heard her; he is very busy with his own
thoughts. She waits a pitiful moment and then bravely goes
over to him and continues.*] So the way I sum it up is that
you can't warm over cold mutton, not unless you're a weak-
ling, and you yourself once said there's nothing uglier than
ex-lovers being friends. . . . So I'm going to say good-
bye, Steven. [*She holds out her hand.*]

GAYE. Good-bye, Linda. [*He takes her hand. He is about to
drop it, and then, something still on his mind, thoughtfully.*]
Listen. . . . Is that all he said—just "I love you?"

LINDA. [*Wide-eyed.*] Yes, Steven. . . .

[GAYE *drops her hand slowly—walks over to the sofa and
sinks down.*]

GAYE. Well! . . . No matter what I do—it seems I can't
escape from comedy! . . . [*A moment, and then suddenly
an idea begins to grow. His face lights up—the old excitement is returning.* LINDA *stands watching him fascinated.
Slowly.*] I think I've got the most exquisitely lyrical
damned idea anybody ever had since Time began! [*Quickly
and on tiptoe* LINDA *walks across to the desk, takes out
notebook and pencil, comes back and sits down.* GAYE *gives
her a swift, absent-minded look. He rises, excited, and
moves across the room. Over his shoulder.*] Ready?

LINDA. [*Pencil poised, a smile beginning to break.*] Ready.

ACCENT ON YOUTH

GAYE. [*Dictating with great excitement.*] Act one. . . .
Scene one. . . . A pent-house apartment in New York
City.—Change that! [*He comes over and sits on the arm
of her chair. He glances at her abstractly.*] The bedroom
. . . of a castle in Spain. . . .

[*As he talks, and as* LINDA *writes,*

THE CURTAIN FALLS

THE END

PROPERTY PLOT

ACT ONE

Small arm chair
Desk
Swivel chair
Wing chair
4-foot console table
Large "Charles" arm chair
Small smoke table
Coffee table
Sofa
Side chair
6-foot console table
Italian console table and urn with bay leaves
ON DESK:
    Large desk blotter
    Small roller blotter
    Ink stand
    Fountain pen
    Cigarette box at both ends of desk
    Matches on upper left end, with ash tray
    Ash tray on lower right end
    Pad of note paper
    Pencil
    Eraser

PROPERTY PLOT

Small piece of statuary
5 manuscripts in lower left corner
Telephone
Paper knife
UNDER DESK:
  Waste paper basket
IN CENTER DRAWER OF DESK:
  Large check book
IN UPPER LEFT DRAWER:
  Passport
  Loose papers
IN UPPER RIGHT DRAWER:
  LINDA's knitting for Act II
ON SMALL SMOKE TABLE:
  Matches and ash tray
ON CONSOLE TABLE LEFT:
  2 wooden carved statues
  Lamp
  Ash trays
ON COFFEE TABLE:
  Tray
  Sherry decanter with stopper off
  3 sherry glasses—2 filled
  Ash tray and matches
  Cigarette box
  3 manuscripts for actors
  Tobacco humidor
BOOK CASE WITH:
  1 globe of the world
  3 framed photographs of women
  Tobacco jar (wooden)

PROPERTY PLOT

4 stacks of manuscripts
2 stacks of magazines
3 large atlases
Bronze head of boy
Over Book Cases:
  4 framed Degas' sketches
  2 wooden figures
  Persian shield
  Wooden carved head of a boy
Over Wing Chair up Right:
  Wall mirror
Over Chair down Right:
  1 Degas sketch
  4 framed autographed photographs
Above Console Table Left:
  Hanging book shelves with
    gaye's nineteen manuscripts bound
    Additional shelves with bound plays
  5 framed wax miniatures
  2 framed fruit water colors
  2 Mosaic placques
On Console Table at Back Right:
  Lamp
  galloway's hat, gloves and umbrella
Off Left:
  Note book for linda
  10 typed letters for linda
  Glass of water
  Pill box
  Manuscript for genevieve

PROPERTY PLOT

ACT TWO

Scene i

Console table
Drum table
Piano
Bench
Small smoke table
Large "Charles" arm chair
Sofa
Swivel chair
Side chair
Desk
Side chair
On Console Table Down Right:
  Lamp
  Vase of Lilacs
  Framed photograph of LINDA
  Telephone
On Drum Table up Right:
  Lamp
On Piano:
  Vase of small yellow flowers
  Ash tray
On Small Smoke Table:
  Ashtray and matches
  GAYE's pipe and tobacco pouch
On Desk:
  Same set up as Act One plus lamp

PROPERTY PLOT

OFF LEFT:
Tray with coffee cup
Jewel case for GAYE

ACT TWO

SCENE 2

Ash tray on piano
Small sprig of yellow flowers loose for GAYE
Lamp shade put back on desk lamp
Photograph replaced

ACT THREE

Same furniture lay-out as Act One
"Charles" chair is at coffee table
Small smoke table is off
Waste basket L. of desk
The curtains are open
ON DESK:
Same as Act One except cigarette box and matches set
upper left corner and ash tray in lower left corner
Notebook
Phone
ON COFFEE TABLE:
Checker board, set for the movements of the game
Cigarette box and matches
FLOGDELL'S untouched drink
Small ash tray at upper end
ON CONSOLE TABLE LEFT (in addition):
Whiskey tray and two glasses

PROPERTY PLOT

    Ash tray with three butts

OFF LEFT:

    Vase of roses

    Bunch of chrysanthemums

    Note for DICKIE

    Coins for GALLOWAY

ELECTRICAL INVENTORY

14—1000 watt spots
6—6 lamps sections of X-ray
1—200 watt spot on stand with slide dimmer
4—sun ray projectors
2—4 lamp strips
3—table lamps
6—1000 watt lekolites (front lights)
2—wall brackets
1—telephone and bell
2—heavy duty switchboards
1—hall lantern

COLORS:

Spots #1—#7—#8—Dark blue
All other spots—double bastard amber-front ring
Fronts—double bastard amber
Sun projectors—light amber
Drop floor units—(pink—light amber—light amber)
Drop overhead units—(pink—light amber—dark blue)
200 watt spot—frost

LIGHT PLOT

ACT ONE

Fronts—full throughout play
Foots—½ up throughout play
X-ray (amber and pink)—⅔ up throughout play
X-ray (blue)—full
Spots—#1—#7—#8—½ up
All other spots—full throughout play
Sun projectors—¾ up
Drop floor units (pink and amber)
Drop overhead units (pink and amber and blue) ¾ up
200 watt spot—¼ up throughout play
Stips—2 lamps on in each—1 white, 1 amber throughout
    play

ACT TWO—I

Same except—
Spots 1— 7— 8—out
X-ray (blue)—out
Sun projectors—½ up
Drop floor units—(amber and blue)—½
Drop overhead units—(pink and amber)—½

LIGHT PLOT

ACT TWO—II

Same except—
Sun projectors—out
Lamps lit
Drop overhead and floor units (blue)—½

ACT THREE

Same except—
Drop overhead and floor units (blue)—full

PUBLICITY THROUGH YOUR LOCAL
PAPERS

The press can be an immense help in giving publicity to your productions. In the belief that the best reviews from the New York and other large papers are always interesting to local audiences, and in order to assist you, we are printing below several excerpts from those reviews.

To these we have also added a number of suggested press notes which may be used either as they stand or changed to suit your own ideas and submitted to the local press.

———

"—Mr. Raphaelson's drama is by all odds the most adroit and most finished comedy the season has revealed. Its writing gives forth a pleasant glow. It is sensitive, intelligent and uncommonly inventive. It touches the heart at the same time that it tickles the risibilities."

New York Evening Post.

"The idea is full of comedy implications—a genuinely captivating play—good-humored and pleasantly insane."

New York Times.

"—One of the season's most delightful items. A comedy of great charm. The reunion of youth and middle age brings to a close a most amusing comedy of moods and manners that is written with dexterity—"

Brooklyn Times-Union.

PUBLICITY NOTES

"A touch of Molnar, a dash of Noel Coward, and a lot of good common sense in story development make this, I think, the happiest romance of the current theatre season."

New York Daily News.

"—A suave and steadily amusing comedy which has both lightness and substance, a comedy, in fact, of gaiety, urbanity and point."

New York Evening Journal.

"—A thoroughly amusing, smart, urbane and sophisticated entertainment."

New York World-Telegram.

"—Gay, ingenious and brilliant comedy."

New York Daily Mirror.

"—Extremely amusing writing—it is gayly sad, sadly gay and very, very wise. Rich and radiant comedy."

New York World-Telegram (2d review).

———

The love of middle-age for youth has been the subject of many books and plays. Indeed there are many who contend that the mature years are the ripest for love at its fullest.

About thirteen years ago, this theory came into being, by way of a book called "The Dangerous Age." It had to do with a woman who had her greatest love affair when she herself had reached the fascinating age of forty. The book created all sorts of excitement and much controversy. Finally it reached the theatre stage.

Much more daring, however, though not so well known, was a play by Bjornson which was called "When the New

Wine Blooms." The heroes of this piece were all men past middle age, and their love affairs involved girls who were the same age as their own daughters.

Fascinated by the same subject that great novelist, Zola, took a fling also at middle-aged love, his novel "Dr. Pascal" showing the hero, an old man, in love with a girl young enough to be his grand-daughter.

Some time later another Frenchman, Henri Bernstein, discussed the same theme in "The Claw" in which Lionel Barrymore did some of the best acting of his career.

Swiftly the years have gone by since these plays and books registered their theories, but recently a new champion appeared who indicated that perfected happiness is possible in middle age. His name was Walter B. Pitkin, and his book "Life Begins at Forty." His propaganda spread like wildfire and his book became the success of the day.

But those enthusiasts who have found Mr. Pitkin's hard facts and authenticated statement impressive, should certainly see "Accent on Youth," which emphasizes the romantic side of the prime of life while paying due credit to youth and its attractions.

Be sure you don't miss this wise and charming comedy when the ————— Players present "Accent on Youth" at ————— Theatre on ————— evening.

———————

The dashing young blades of our city had better watch out after "Accent on Youth" is presented by the ————— Players. For here they will learn that middle-aged men have a charm and a way with the girls that is based on a deep appreciation of the sex that only ripe experience can bestow. Against the impetuosity of youth will be shown the urbanity of maturity and the warmer understanding that comes with years.

There are some girls who like to take awkward youth and mould it into their idea of manhood. But, on the other hand, there are those girls who prefer the finished product to be found among men of forty and over.

Such men seem to know how to please a lovely female whether it be his manner in holding her coat or his task in selecting the flower to match her dress and personality. They know human frailty, especially the feminine sort and they look upon the lady's shortcomings with humor and understanding.

With all this in view the ———— Players take this occasion to beseech you to see this charming play. It will refresh you with its quips and ingenious literary twists. It will convince you that the Fountain of Youth can be found at the ———— Theatre on ———— evening when they present "Accent on Youth."

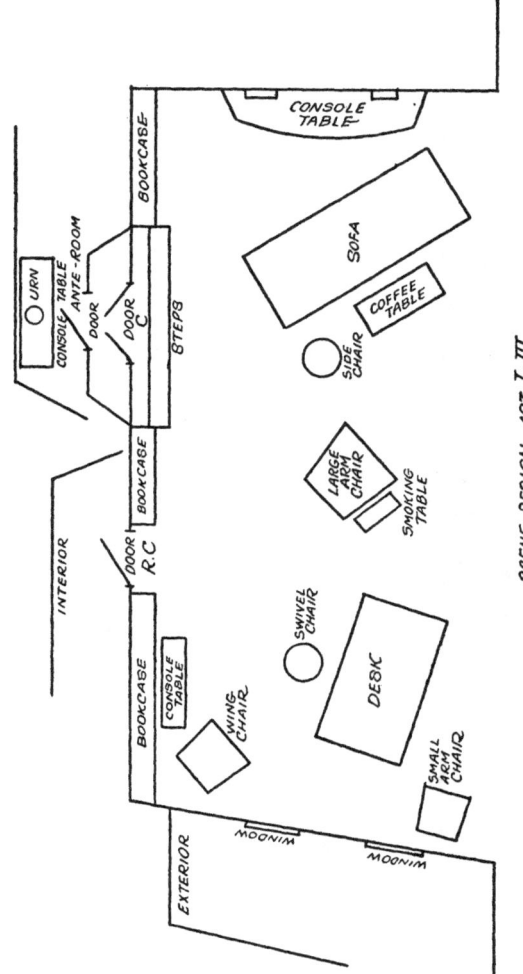

SCENE DESIGN ACT I-III
"ACCENT ON YOUTH"

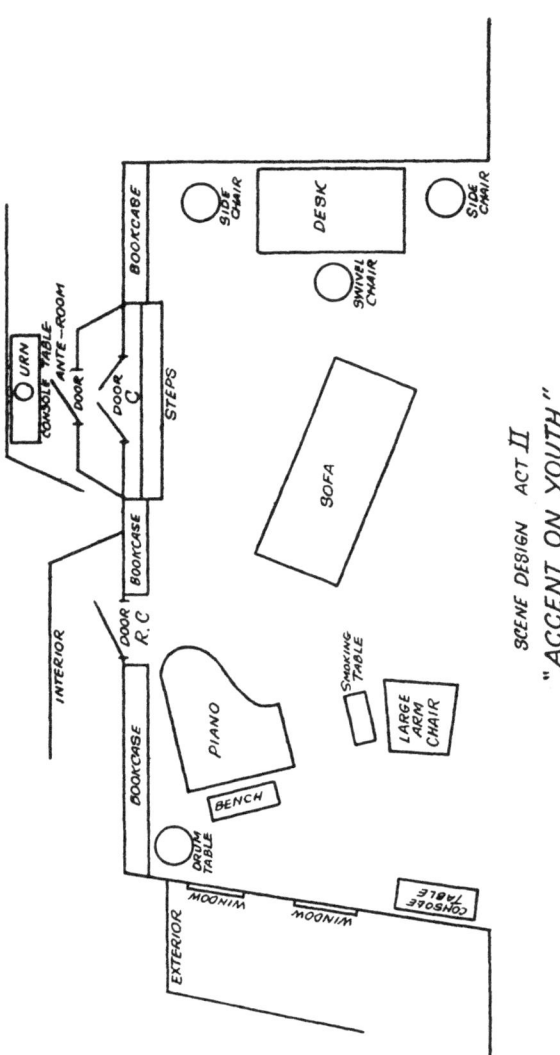

SCENE DESIGN ACT II
"ACCENT ON YOUTH"

OTHER TITLES AVAILABLE FROM SAMUEL FRENCH

EURYDICE
Sarah Ruhl

Dramatic Comedy / 5m, 2f / Unit Set

In *Eurydice*, Sarah Ruhl reimagines the classic myth of Orpheus through the eyes of its heroine. Dying too young on her wedding day, Eurydice must journey to the underworld, where she reunites with her father and struggles to remember her lost love. With contemporary characters, ingenious plot twists, and breathtaking visual effects, the play is a fresh look at a timeless love story.

"RHAPSODICALLY BEAUTIFUL. A weird and wonderful new play - an inexpressibly moving theatrical fable about love, loss and the pleasures and pains of memory."
- *The New York Times*

"EXHILARATING!! A luminous retelling of the Orpheus myth, lush and limpid as a dream where both author and audience swim in the magical, sometimes menacing, and always thrilling flow of the unconscious."
- *The New Yorker*

"Exquisitely staged by Les Waters and an inventive design team... Ruhl's wild flights of imagination, some deeply affecting passages and beautiful imagery provide transporting pleasures. They conspire to create original, at times breathtaking, stage pictures."
- *Variety*

"Touching, inventive, invigoratingly compact and luminously liquid in its rhythms and design, *Eurydice* reframes the ancient myth of ill-fated love to focus not on the bereaved musician but on his dead bride – and on her struggle with love beyond the grave as both wife and daughter."
- *The San Francisco Chronicle*

SAMUELFRENCH.COM

OTHER TITLES AVAILABLE FROM SAMUEL FRENCH

EVIL DEAD: THE MUSICAL

Book & Lyrics By George Reinblatt
Music By Frank Cipolla/Christopher Bond/Melissa Morris/
George Reinblatt

Musical Comedy / 6m, 4f / Unit set

Based on Sam Raimi's 80s cult classic films, *Evil Dead* tells the tale of 5 college kids who travel to a cabin in the woods and accidentally unleash an evil force. And although it may sound like a horror, its not! The songs are hilariously campy and the show is bursting with more farce than a Monty Python skit. *Evil Dead: The Musical* unearths the old familiar story: boy and friends take a weekend getaway at abandoned cabin, boy expects to get lucky, boy unleashes ancient evil spirit, friends turn into Candarian Demons, boy fights until dawn to survive. As musical mayhem descends upon this sleepover in the woods, "camp" takes on a whole new meaning with up-roarious numbers like "All the Men in my Life Keep Getting Killed by Candarian Demons," "Look Who's Evil Now" and "Do the Necronomicon."

Outer Critics Circle nomination for
Outstanding New Off-Broadway Musical

"The next Rocky Horror Show!"
- *New York Times*

"A ridiculous amount of fun."
- *Variety*

"Wickedly campy good time."
- *Associated Press*